The Document Matters

Responses to
Abnormal Man

"Grant's fans will never forgive him."
—Penguin Group, Senior Executive Editor

"There is some dark magic in this one. I mean, really dark. Like whittle-my-bones-to-a-bloody-point dark. Jerkins calmly, unflinchingly goes about his business of crafting some troubled yet sympathetic characters who are in dire straits. That he manages to make these characters sympathetic, their problems understandable, is impressive and prompts the reader to consider the justice in violence. But despite the skill of its execution...I must pass."
—HarperCollins, Acquisitions Editor

"I'm afraid that I really didn't like it. While it is certainly well-written, as are all of Grant's books, I found it to be too dark and off-putting. There really isn't anyone to 'root' for and the subject matter is pretty distasteful. That being said, I would hate to end our publishing relationship with Grant at this point. For me, personally, and as a company as well, we are really committed to building Grant's career."
—Penguin/Berkley (prior to ending
their publishing relationship with the author)

ABNORMAL MAN

ALSO BY GRANT JERKINS

A Very Simple Crime
At the End of the Road
The Ninth Step
Done in One

ABNORMAL MAN

OR

THE MIDDLE GROUND

Being a School Compendium in the Scriptural Style
Of Criminology and the Abnormal Classes
And Giving an Honest Account and Was Thereby Raised Up

By

That Ancient Servant of Christ

GRANT JERKINS

ABC Group Documentation
an imprint of Down & Out Books
3959 Van Dyke Rd, Ste. 265
Lutz, FL 33558
www.DownAndOutBooks.com

Cover photograph by jw lawson
Cover design by chad m pelton

ISBN: 1-943402-39-6
ISBN-13: 978-1-943402-39-7

For ZKJ

Note:

All epigrams and extracts—as well as this book's title—are taken from the Bureau of Education Circular of Information No. 4, *Abnormal Man, Being Essays on Education and Crime and Related Subjects*, by Arthur MacDonald, Government Printing Office, Washington, D.C., 1893. In addition, the author is indebted to the Sub-Sub Programmer who kept dark hours alone with her loupe and logarithms to amass, correlate, scan, and furthermore write proprietary code to digitally capture *le mots justes* contained therein—the very phrases that would illume, limn, and inform the following narrative. She did this on the author's behalf, requesting in return, only anonymity. Fare thee well, poor devil of a Sub-Sub.

For the convenience of those who are interested in questions concerning the abnormal classes—including their moral, intellectual, and physical education—the author presents in book form a number of his writings...In doing this the author has temporarily taken the point of view of the subject of each study, avoiding criticism, so that the reader may gain a clear insight...

BILLY

The Moon.

You keep swallowing and you're not sure why. You can feel your Adam's apple bobbing up and down, up and down, over and over. Your eyes are closed, and there is a diffuse white glow bleeding through your eyelids. A pleasant, welcoming light. Not the sun. No, it is not the sun. It is the moon. Yes, the moon.

When you were still just a little kid, you believed—*certain, you were absolutely certain*—that the moon followed you. You can remember being in the backseat of your father's restored Chevelle SS, driving home from a vacation in Gatlinburg, and watching the moon through the blue-green glass of the side window.

The moon stays with you. It follows you. No matter how fast the car speeds down the highway, that magnetic white disc keeps up with you, never lagging behind.

At first you think it might be some kind of optical illusion, some trick you aren't yet old enough to understand, so you test the theory by looking away from it for a little while. Maybe it just seems like the moon is following you because you never take your eyes off it. A clock's hands can only be seen to move if you take your eyes away from it for a little while. It's only when you look back later that you can tell the hands have changed position. Maybe if you ignore the moon for a little while, maybe when you look back at it again, you will be able to tell it is really getting farther away. That it isn't really following you after all.

So you look up front at the silver, rectangular radio buttons. They are the old-fashioned mechanical kind that you have to stab with your finger to make the dial physically turn to the preset station. The green radium-like glow of the dashboard instrument panel bathes the car's interior, like being in a submarine. Sixty miles an hour. The car is moving at sixty miles an hour. Your daddy's face does not look sinister in that green glow, but instead it looks warm and safe. You didn't know it then, but he was your real daddy. Your true daddy. Not the son-of-a-bitch replacement. And your mama reaches back over the seat and scratches your knee with her long red fingernails and says your name real soft. "Billy? You awake, sweetie?" But you don't answer her. Just let her think you're asleep. And you watch her take her hand away and rest it high on Daddy's leg, nestled in the crotch.

And it feels good seeing that. You feel good. Because you have no way of knowing that she will be dead in nine years.

And it has been long enough to test your theory. To see if it is real. You turn your head and look back out the side window, holding your breath in anticipation. And it's true. The moon is still there. In the exact same place. This car is rolling down the road at sixty miles per hour, so the moon should be far, far behind you, but it has not slowed down one little bit. It's following you. *You.*

For the rest of the trip, you continue to test the moon. When the car stops, the moon stops too. It waits right there in the sky. It waits for you to get moving again. And when the car turns, the moon turns with it. Sometimes it ends up following you from the other side of the car, but it never stops following.

It is following you.

Your name is Billy Smith and that is not a special name. It is common.

But the moon follows you.

And that makes you special.

You are special.

You haven't seen the moon—or the sun—in more than three months. But still, all these years later, you know it is out there, waiting for you. You can feel it. Throbbing with gravity, pulling at you. Waiting for you.

There are no windows in this place, only fluorescent lights that stay on all day, all night. This place is not a prison, but really it is. The Grierson Holding and Processing Facility for Violent Offenders. Not a prison.

You ask yourself: How did it happen? Can you really be responsible for this? And you look around yourself and realize that every decision you have ever made in your life has brought you to this time, to this place. You are where you are supposed to be.

You are eighteen years old.

Was there a choice? Was there ever really a choice? Or was this all preordained? From the moment your head crowned from between your mother's splayed legs, had all of this already been decided for you? Written down? Or was it chaos?

No. It was choice. Of course it was. Of course. A never-ending series of decisions. More choices than there are numbers. Every step was decided upon. Chosen. How could you have not realized that?

It was all a choice.

Swallowing. You keep swallowing. Why? Is it nerves? Anticipation? The light that surrounds you is too warm and intense to be the moon. The blunt white light that bleeds through your closed lids is implacable. Waiting patiently for you to open your eyes. And you do. You swallow one last time and open your eyes.

You are staring into the dead flat eye of a video camera. Static. It is waiting for you to speak. There are three softbox lights on tripods angled around you, lighting you for the camera.

The woman's motorcycle helmet rests on the scratched and dirty table here in the not-a-prison interview room. The helmet is black, an impenetrable orb. And on the back, in red spray paint, the anarchy symbol. The letter *A* bursting through a ragged circle that can't contain it.

The woman is staring at you. Her camera is staring at you. You can hear it humming, waiting. The fuzzy black boom mic is pointing at you, accusatory. You like the woman, and you have agreed to speak to her. To be in her movie. Her documentary. About you.

You want to tell her about how when you were just a little kid you used to think the moon followed you. In fact, you open your mouth and you are about to say that very thing, but you don't. Because it would be a lie. The truth is that you still think that the moon follows you. And you always will.

JAYMES

You wonder why someone would name their baby girl Jaymes and then be upset when, years later, she announces that she's a lesbian. It's like they prearranged it. Jaymes. What kind of name is that to saddle a child with? It is the name you give your daughter when what you really wanted was a son.

You are eighteen years old, and when you left your parents' house this morning, it was for the last time. You are never going back. You have your motorcycle—*hello, Dad, your daughter is named Jaymes and she rides a bad motorscooter.* *Wake up*—you have jeans, T-shirts, underwear, socks, comb, and a toothbrush crammed in your backpack. *No makeup, obvious clue number three. The clichés just keep piling up.* And you have your digital video camera. The camera is the only reason you stayed there as long as you did. That camera cost you every cent you ever made asking people if they wanted to supersize that order.

You look at the boy sitting across from you, and you realize that is all that he is. A boy. He is eighteen years old, same as you, but he looks like he is about twelve. Thin to the point of emaciation. Skin like dirty chalk. He is pitiful. You have never felt a maternal impulse in your life, but you are overwhelmed with a need to grab this boy up and hug him and cover him in kisses. If you gave in to such a ludicrous temptation, you would need to be careful of your razor blade earrings. The kid has the complexion of a hemophiliac.

The kid. His name is Billy, and you have been following his story in the *Atlanta Journal Constitution*, on CNN, the Faux News Network, and the various blogs that have erupted around Billy Smith and what he has done.

You do not know why your interest in the case rose to the level of obsession, but it did. It seemed to somehow mirror the arc of your own life. The snowball effect of bad choices, choices that often weren't choices at all. The mocking echo of a life out of control.

You are eighteen. An adult. You have been making films your whole life. Films about yourself. You have chronicled your life. And posted your images and rants online. But now you are ready to turn the camera around. Now you are ready to do something real.

BILLY

"Another two hours of shrugging isn't going to help me."

You shrug again. The camera intimidates you. The girl doesn't, but the camera does. You think the girl is kind of cool. You like the pink stubble like a neon nimbus around her head, the piercings. The tattoos. Her tattoos are not like Frank's. You can tell hers were professionally done.

You lift your hands to your mouth and chew a hangnail on your thumb. You have to lift both hands at the same time because they are cuffed together. They allowed you to do these interviews, but only with certain conditions. Like the guards standing in the corners. And the handcuffs.

Not-a-prison.

"I'm sure it's nice to get out of population and chew on your hands for two hours, but, you know what? You're wasting my time."

There is nothing to say. What can you say?

"A lot of people care about this."

She is not looking at you directly, but watching your image in the monitor.

You speak.

"I've always been with Frank."

9

BILLY

It is science class and you are looking at a Canadian travel pamphlet while the teacher speaks. You do not remember when you first became fascinated with Canada, but you are. Everything in Canada is green. Or cold and white and pure. You really do not even remember where you got the stack of Canadian tourist brochures that you carry around with you in your backpack. You have had them for so long that they are wrinkled and corner-bumped and the glossy photographs are missing thumbprint-size hunks of color.

There is a loud crack, like a gunshot, and your head jerks up. It was the sound of a book hitting the floor.

"Who remembers Newton's third law of motion?"

A girl raises her hand and says, "For every action there is an equal and opposite reaction."

"Correct. I pushed the book forward and it fell off my desk. The action was pushing. The equal and opposite reaction was that the book moved forward. The foreseeable consequence of the action and reaction was that the book fell to the floor."

The teacher picks up the book and holds it out to the class as though it were a newly discovered and potentially dangerous vertebrate.

"According to the concept of Chaos Theory, in any sufficiently complex environment, any action, even a

11

simple one, will create a series of chain reactions that are unforeseen and unpredictable."

The teacher looks at you now. You close your textbook to hide the brochure you were looking at.

"A butterfly flaps its wings in China, and six weeks later a hurricane forms off the coast of Florida. You can't foresee that. Or, for instance, I didn't know that by pushing the book and it falling and smacking the floor, that young Master Billy here would wake up and join the class. That was unforeseen. And could this unforeseen outcome set off a chain reaction? Perhaps the startling sound will leave Billy a bit more alert when he leaves here. And maybe that alertness will cause him to be aware of his environment in a way he would not otherwise have been. Maybe he'll make decisions that will impact the rest of his day. Or the rest of his life. Or maybe he'll just remember not to daydream in class. It is unforeseeable. And that's the point."

You are bright red. You don't like attention of any kind.

A boy in the back raises his hand. He is a smart boy and does not mind drawing attention to himself.

"If the sequence of events is untraceable, then how do we know the events share a cause-and-effect relationship? How do we know the hurricane wouldn't have happened anyway?"

"We don't. And that's a good point. So you, Hunter, fall into the *Is it chaos or is it fate?* camp. And that's reasonable. Chaos theory is just that. A theory. Of course fate, as a theory, doesn't hold much water either. That's worth keeping in mind. But let's assume—for the moment—that chaos is indeed a valid theory. Now let's look at it on a global scale. If our action is to cut down all the world's rainforests, what are the possible reactions?"

"A greenhouse effect. Global warming."

"Maybe. Probably."

"The ozone hole over the Antarctic could get even bigger."

"Maybe"

"We lose possible cures for AIDS and cancer."

"Maybe."

"We speed up the return of the Ice Age."

"Could be."

You do not offer an answer. You never speak in class unless forced.

"Maybe, maybe, maybe. See, we really don't know what the reaction will be, but we're pretty sure it ain't gonna be good. It's a question of control, of which we have very little."

Someone, the smart kid, asks, "But if we can anticipate, don't we have control? In the microcosm of this classroom, couldn't we have anticipated every possible reaction of your action of pushing the book to the floor?"

"No. Even in this closed environment, the possibilities are beyond number. When scientists were preparing to detonate the first atomic bomb, many of them believed a chain of reactions would ignite the atmosphere. *Ignite the atmosphere.* Think about that. But they went ahead and did it, didn't they?"

The bell rings, but you stay seated because the teacher is still talking and you want to hear the rest of this.

"So, anyway, the next time you toss out an old

newspaper or throw away an aluminum can without recycling it, remember Chaos Theory. For your every action, you set off a chain of events beyond control. Think about it."

You follow the last of the other students out the door and you hear the teacher say, "See ya', Billy." You half lift your hand in acknowledgement, but you don't turn around.

Outside the classroom, two bigger boys run down the hall, weaving through the crowd. As they rush past you, one of them slams you into the wall, and the other slaps the books out of your arms. Already halfway down the hall, one of them calls back to you over his shoulder, "Buggie!" Then they both emit high-pitched giggles that sound like jungle animals.

You gather the books up and put them in your backpack. You should have done that before you left class, but that would have taken too much time and the teacher might have tried to have a conversation with you. Teachers are always trying to engage you in conversation. And when they do that, it makes your stomach hurt. And your stomach hurts right now. It hurts bad. It always hurts bad before you have to see Mrs. Hamby. And you do not think that you can endure both the meeting and the pain at the same time. You need to ease the hurt.

The hall has emptied, and you have ten minutes before your meeting with the school psychologist. You head for the boys bathroom.

You take the last stall, the handicapped one. This is

your favorite not because it is the biggest, but because the lock on it still works and because it is directly under the overhead ventilation fan.

You unroll a handful of toilet paper from the dispenser. You already know the perfect amount. You wad it up into a ball about the size of a rodent brain with a bit angling off from it like a brainstem. You will hold it from the brainstem.

From your jeans pocket you extract a yellow Bic lighter, stolen from your stepfather, Harvey Peruro. You set the toilet paper rodent brain afire. The trick is to get a clean burn so that there is no smoke. Regardless of the ventilation fan, if there is smoke, it will permeate the bathroom and give you away. You watch the flame take hold, and as soon as it does, the pain in your stomach vanishes. You do not know if it is simply that you forget about the pain, or if fire acts as a painkiller. It doesn't matter. The flame is beautiful, calming. It pulsates like an orange rose. A burning blossom. A fire flower.

And then, still standing over the toilet, you use your other hand to unbuckle and drop your pants, push down your underwear, and it feels good to have your genitals exposed to the air. No shame. No self-consciousnesses.

You know your cock is kind of small. From gym class and the mandatory showers. Most of the boys your age have bodies of substance. Bodies thick with bulk and muscle or lean with speed and innate strength. Pendulous penises that sway with weighty arrogance from strange dense growths of dark pubic hair as they walk around the locker room.

Your pubic hair only just started to come in last summer. Harvey seems to enjoy referring to you as a late bloomer, and the few times that a drinking buddy of his comes to the house, Harvey inevitably points out that you are a late bloomer so as to explain your skinny pale body and voice that has only a hint of masculine timbre. It all seemed to start around the same time all the stuff with your mother happened. You just kind of stopped growing. The doctor called it delayed puberty. They are supposed to start giving you hormone shots, but then the doctor said that could exacerbate the conduct disorder. And you've been held back a couple of grades. Learning disability stemming from emotional trauma. Again, the stuff with your mom. You kind of have a lot of problems.

And so you have only a little bit of pubic hair that has sprung up in two modest patches, each about the size of a quarter, around the base of your dick. The hair is so fine that the light has to hit it just right in order to be seen. In the locker room you keep your back to the other boys because you do not want them to point out the smooth hairless contrast of your boyish body to the sprouting mannishness of theirs.

And in fear and embarrassment and shame your scrotum shrivels, your testicles attempt to crawl up into your groin, and your penis shrinks down and draws itself into nothing more than a tiny cap. And as often as you can, you will busy yourself at your locker. Unlacing your shoes as slowly as possible. Pulling your socks off so that you have to stop and turn them right side out. And as the other boys emerge from the showers and discard their towels into the wire hamper, you grab one and pretend to clean a spot from your shoe and then you pretend that you have already been through the shower and you are drying your body with the gray towel and you have not had to endure the humiliation of the shower, the degrading walk across the locker room. But often you do. You do have to face it.

But now, in the handicapped stall, with fire in your right hand, you look down and your cock is rock hard. So hard it is pointing straight up, almost touching your belly. And it doesn't look so small now. Now it looks big. And your balls are hanging pendulums underneath. They feel as though they have weight. Substance. That they are *there*. And they therefore give you weight and substance. You are *here*.

And all it takes is two strokes. Two strokes and it explodes. Your cum is watery, like pee, but it is there. Before this past summer, when you did this nothing came out. But now you can cum. Ejaculate. And you see droplets of thin semen jump higher than the burning paper which has burned itself down to the brainstem. You have left the end of the brainstem unraveled, flat, a sort of neural net, and you let the flame touch your fingers before you drop it. You have timed it right. The flame consumes the last of the paper during its lazy drop to the toilet bowl. No smoke. A clean burn. Perfect.

You pull your pants and underwear back up, buckle your belt. You use toilet paper to clean the spilled body fluid from the rim of the toilet, and you flush everything away. You watch the ash and your semen swirl together and then disappear.

You take a minute and lean against the stall door. And you think the thought that you always think after you do this. From your favorite book. The book you have read probably seventy times. You will never forget picking that book from the returns cart at the school library. *Fahrenheit 451,* by Ray Bradbury. An illustration of a paper man engulfed by flames was on the cover. And you opened the book. And you read the first line.

It was a pleasure to burn.

And your body just kind of went into a state of numb ecstasy. Because it was true. It was the truest sentence that had ever been written. That ever will be written.

It was a pleasure to burn.

The hall in the administrative wing is quiet. You don't like the loudness of students, but you also do not like the unnatural absence of sound you find here. It reminds you of doctors' offices. You are missing Ms. Wiggins's English class to be here, and that is the one class you kind of like. She has you reading Stephen Crane. *The Red Badge of Courage.* And also some poetry by him. There is a poem about a guy who eats his own heart and hates the way it tastes, and another one about bastard mushrooms that grow in polluted blood. It's pretty badass stuff. Hardcore. You stop at a door with the word *Counselor* stenciled on it.

Inside is a small waiting room. You still have a few minutes, so you sit and wait. After a minute, the counselor's door opens and a girl steps out. Beth Andrews. A cutter. You are not privy to gossip or inside information, but the knowledge that Beth Andrews is a cutter is so widespread that it has filtered down to even the lowest rungs of the social ladder, so you know what Beth Andrews is. Just as she knows what you are. Just as everybody in the school knows what you are.

Mrs. Hamby is all right. She looks nice. Poofy hair. Her perfume smells like bug spray. Raid. You are not here voluntarily. This is not a free choice. You are here as a result of other choices you have made in the past. This is a reaction to your actions. A consequence.

"How's it going, Billy?"

"Okay, I guess."

"Great. No problems?"

You shrug your shoulders and shake your head.

It always starts this way. Mrs. Hamby doesn't really want there to be any problems. Not because she cares about you, but because if there are problems, then she will have to do something about it. In the end, it is better for both of you if you pretend that your life is all *Little House on the Prairie* and shit and she pretends that she doesn't know you're lying.

"Excellent. You getting along okay at work? Your family?"

You nod to indicate that yes, yes your life is one of rosy-cheeked wholesome goodness.

"No more problems with your stepfather?"

An image pops into your head. Of Harvey, standing over you, fists clenched, spit spraying from his mouth as he yells at you. *I'm glad your mother died. She'd be ashamed to know what a weak little pussy she has for a son. Fucking faggot.*

You shake your head and say, "Harvey's all right."

Mrs. Hamby smiles and nods with satisfaction. "And if you see he's getting angry, what should you do?"

You picture yourself lying face down on the filthy carpet of your bedroom, your arms cradling your head, shielding yourself from the blows raining down.

"Sit down and talk it out," you say.

"Good. And if that doesn't work?"

And you see yourself running down the street of your neighborhood at night. Blood from a cut on your forehead streams into your eye, stinging.

"I leave the house. Give him a chance to cool off. Give us both a chance to get our thoughts together."

"Excellent!" Mrs. Hamby beams. So far this recital is going perfectly. Not a note has been missed. "And what about your job? Do you think it's working out?"

You see yourself in the kitchen at Shoney's. Sid, the assistant cook, stands too close to you, invading your space. *If you're not my friend, then you must be my enemy,* Sid says. So you dig in your pocket and come up with a damp, wadded five-dollar-bill. This is all the money you have. Sid pockets the bill and says friends help each other out.

"Oh, yeah," you say to Mrs. Hamby, "I like working." You look down at your feet and see that there is a baby cockroach on your shoe. Just sitting there. No wonder the office smells like Raid.

Mrs. Hamby opens your file and reads from a report. "Your Job Coach says she's in the fading stage. That she's phased out the onsite visits. You're independent now. They say that work is the best therapy. And it's true. It gives you—it gives me—a sense of fulfillment."

You are still looking at the baby cockroach sitting on your shoe. It has a whitish stripe near the head. You know that a baby cockroach is called a nymph. You wonder if Mrs. Hamby's office is infested.

"Do you know what Teddy Roosevelt said about

work? He said 'Far and away the best prize that life offers is the chance to work hard at work worth doing.' I've always put a lot of stock in that. Well, I know you have to catch your bus. And you work tonight, so I won't keep you."

You stand and head for the door.

"Oh, and, uh, no more incidents with, uhm, fire?"

"No ma'am."

"And you're still taking the meds Dr. Stein prescribed? The uh..." She references your file again. "The olanzapine and sodium valproate?"

You nod your head, but those pills made you sick.

You don't need pills. You know how to make yourself feel better.

"Bye, Mrs. Hamby."

"Bye-bye, now."

You open the office door.

"Billy?"

You don't turn around, but you do pause in the doorway.

"Just remember that I'm here to help. No matter what. No matter how big or how small the problem. Come to me. Okay?"

You look down and see the nymph crawl off your shoe and escape through the open door. You scurry out after it.

BILLY

You step off the school bus into bright sunshine. It hurts your eyes. This is your city. Marietta, Georgia. This is your neighborhood. The houses all look alike. Split-level homes shored up in laminate siding, each painted in one of three shades of powdery pastel—lime, lemon, and orange sherbet. The yards are withered, the Georgia sun having assaulted the earth, robbing it of even its last drop of moisture. The lawns are heaved and depressed where the ground has split open, waiting for water. Towering pine trees bleed pungent sap like stigmata. This is home. This is where you live.

None of the houses are kept up particularly well, but yours stands out as being in the direst state of disrepair. The yellow siding is spotted with long-dead colonies of black mold. The deceased lawn looks worse than the others because it had been long uncut before it succumbed to the heat. Now it looks like the matted beard of a homeless man.

You go in through the carport, and the neighbor's dog, Harley, follows you inside. Harley is some kind of mutt, looks like he has a little bit of Beagle in him, maybe some Collie. His untrimmed claws click on the kitchen floor as he jumps around, happy to see you. You let him lick your face. The dog loves you. You try to get him calm before Harvey hears him, but it is too late.

"You didn't let that goddamn stray into the house, did you? 'Cause if you did, I'll shoot it!"

You try to quiet the dog. "Shh. Shh. It's okay, boy. Shh. Shh. Sorry Harvey!"

Good old Harvey. All-American dad. Technically your stepfather. The man your mother married two years before her diagnosis. Harvey is different now since she died. But you are too.

You can just picture him, sprawled out on his burnt-orange recliner, beer in hand, Judge Judy doling out justice on the TV. He is probably on his third or fourth beer by now—well within the safety zone. Harvey keeps an Igloo cooler parked next to the recliner. Each day he stocks it with a case of Natural Light and a ten-pound bag of ice purchased from the Citgo station up the street. Harvey also keeps an empty plastic milk jug within easy reach. The beer runs through him so quick that it would require far too many trips to the bathroom to relieve his bladder. At one time, he kept a dishtowel draped over the gallon jug for the sake of appearance, but he has long since given up any pretense of discretion. In fact, he sometimes asks you to empty it for him. He is that lazy. That particular chore physically sickens you. What is most bothersome about it is not the fact that it is someone's pee, but that the container is usually still warm with Harvey's body heat. It feels alive.

You find a leftover piece of Kentucky Fried Chicken in the refrigerator and toss it out onto the carport so that the dog will run out after it.

In the living room, Harvey has set his tableau as you imagined it. As it always is. Without deviation.

After your mother was diagnosed, the *Marietta Daily Journal* did a story about her rare form of cancer and how your family did not have health insurance. And even though you have never been to church in your life, The First Baptist Church of Christ started a community-wide fundraising campaign. When people went to Kroger to grocery shop, the cashier would ask them if they would like to donate a dollar or five dollars or a ten spot to the Janet Peruro-Smith Fund. They would get a little yellowish-pink piece of construction paper cut in the shape of a peach and the cashier would put the person's name on it and tape it to the front window and before long the whole damn street-facing window of the Cobb Parkway Kroger was covered with little paper peaches. The front of the store was dim as a cave. You do not know how much money was collected, but Harvey has not worked since the check was presented to him in a little ceremony at the Cobb County Community Center. You remember watching white-haired church ladies mix a huge bowl of red punch made out of Tahitian Treat, cherry Kool-Aid, ginger ale, lime sherbet, and a five-pound bag of sugar. You could actually feel the stuff penetrate the enamel on your teeth. You drank so much of it that you threw up. It looked like you were vomiting blood.

"I have to work today," you tell Harvey.

Harvey doesn't take his eyes off Judge Judy.

"Oh, yeah?"

"Can you take me?"

Harvey pinches the bridge of his nose and his brow creases. He looks as though you have asked him to delineate Stephen Hawking's theorem regarding gravitational singularities within the framework of general relativity, or to maybe say a few words in regards to the black hole information paradox.

Harvey lets go of his unusually broad nasal bridge and says, "Christ, I suppose," but he postulates nothing pertaining to quantum physics.

Harvey retrieves a book nestled between the beer cooler and pee jug. You recognize it immediately. You checked it out from the school library.

"I ought to make your ass stay home. Found this under your bed."

The book is called *The Underground Guide to Teenage Sexuality.*

"You went in my room? Spying?"

Harvey raises one of his puffy, alcohol-infused hands and you flinch.

"I'm all the family you got. Got to take care of you." He fires up a Marlboro Light with his green Bic. "You're so fucking weird. Thought you were on drugs. Turns out you're just, well, what are you, Billy? You turning into some kind of homo?"

"No."

"Don't have to be ashamed. Natural to be curious about sex. Boy your age. Had any experience?"

You shake your head. *This is awful. This is awful. This is awful.*

"Know how to jack off? All guys do it"

This is awful.

Harvey takes a deep drag off his Marlboro Light and ashes cascade over his swollen belly.

"You want, I can show you. Teach you."

You shake your head. This is the worst thing ever.

You want to fold in on yourself, to crumple and disappear. What is Harvey thinking?

"Let me show you."

"No!" You scream at Harvey. And just that quick he is out of his chair. For a lazy overweight drunk, the man can move when the situation calls for it. Quantum physics in action. Watch and learn. He hits you in the offending orifice—your mouth—and your bottom lip splits open like a bag of Jiffy Pop.

"You little faggot!"

Harvey raises his fist to land another blow, but he notices that in the commotion, he has overturned his pee jug and warm urine is hiccupping onto the dirty carpet. As Harvey turns to set it right, you run from the room.

"Next you'll be sucking dicks and wetting the bed," he calls out after you, but you are out the back door. You are gone. You will walk to work or maybe hitch a ride.

BILLY

The dinner rush is crazy tonight. It's Friday and half of Marietta wants to treat itself to an evening of fine dining at Shoney's.

The kitchen trashcans are already overflowing and the manager has asked you and Frank to empty them. Behind the restaurant, you watch Frank manhandle a fifty-gallon trashcan over his head and tilt the barrel over the rim of the dumpster. The gloppy leftovers and kitchen scraps slop into the bin. Frank walks back to where you are still struggling to drag your can toward the dumpster.

Frank walks with a limp. It's not a bad limp, but still, there is something clearly off when he moves. You are pretty sure Frank has an artificial leg. He wears boots and jeans every day, but one time he was reaching to the top shelf of the walk-in refrigerator and his pant leg rode up high, above the black boot, above the white sock, just enough for you to see a crescent of skin. Only it wasn't skin at all. It was some kind of flesh-colored plastic. Not real.

Frank takes the trash barrel from you and empties it into the dumpster.

"You'll need more muscle than that if you're gonna hitch to Canada."

You have told Frank that you are leaving tonight. You are the busboy here, and the waitresses give you a percentage of their tips for keeping the tables clean. You are taking whatever you get tonight and you are leaving. Gone. This will be all the money you will have since Harvey keeps your earnings for your "college fund."

Frank is somewhere in his twenties. An adult, but still young enough that you find yourself drawn to him. He has long black hair that looks like he doesn't wash it very often. And tattoos. Frank has tattoos. On his arms, on his chest. His neck. His face. Like something tribal. You really like Frank, and even though Frank doesn't talk very much, you get the feeling he likes you, too. You have never in your life had a friend. Not a real friend. You want Frank to be your friend.

He stares at your split lip and you cover it with your hand.

"I walked into a door."

"Yeah. Children are God's gift to us. Not everyone understands that."

You feel offended because you think Frank has called you a child. But of course you do look like a child. You look like you are eleven or twelve. The delayed puberty thing. Hormones. Frank can see that he has somehow said something wrong. He unfastens two buttons on his cook's smock (exposing even more blue black prison ink) and reaches in and pulls out a silver medallion on a chain.

"What is it?"

"Saint Christopher. Patron saint of travelers. Protects you."

Frank works the chain over his head and drops it in your hand. You thank him and put it around your neck. You don't know what to say.

Frank lights a cigarette. He smokes Marlboro Lights, just like Harvey.

"I wouldn't mind going to Canada."

Is Frank saying that he wants to go with you?

"Why don't you?"

"Can't. On parole."

"Oh."

You stare at the tattoos that sprawl up and down Frank's muscled arms, over his corded neck, and onto his face. You don't know much about tattoos, but you know enough to know that these crude monochrome words and images were most likely done in prison. The blues and blacks of ink scavenged from ballpoint pens. You see crosses and half a swastika. Satanic symbols. Biblical verses. Spiders. Snakes. Crude renderings of naked women. White supremacist slogans. Pleas for racial equality. Music groups: *Black Sabbath. Slayer. Mayhem. Cannibal Corpse.*

"What did you do?"

Frank crushes the cigarette under his boot and inspects a cross tattoo on his forearm.

"Trusted the wrong person."

Mrs. Hamby got you the busboy job. It is supposed to teach you interaction skills like how to get along well with others. You wonder why Mr. Trapnell, the manager, hires parolees and juvenile delinquents. There must be some kind of tax write-off. Tonight, Trapnell has pulled you off the floor and into the kitchen. The old Hispanic dishwasher got mad about something and walked off the job. (Trapnell is big on immigrant labor, too.) There are gray plastic bus pans stacked along the stainless steel counter, stacked damn near to the ceiling and overflowing with filthy dishes and silverware.

A metallic hose dangles from the ceiling, and you spray it onto the splashguard behind the sink, watching your steamy smeared reflection in the stainless steel. You lose yourself in it. You vaguely hear the crash of a full bus pan being slammed down.

"...Billy. Earth to Billy. Billy, are you there? Earth to Billy."

And you release the trigger of the spray hose and turn around; and Eva, a waitress that you like, says, "You know that's wasteful. People are chopping down rainforests to heat that water."

"Sorry."

"Plus, you're getting a little behind here," she says and indicates the cliff of dirty dishes. She reaches across the counter and pats your cheek. "Focus."

You start scraping nasty, cold, half-eaten food off plates and into the trash can. You load a plastic dishwasher tray full of them and then use the hose to spray scalding hot water over the tray of dirty dishes, to rinse them of congealed grease and clinging food scraps before you shove the full tray along the metal rollers and into the aluminum box that is the automatic dishwasher. The wash cycle takes ninety seconds, and when the dishes come out the other side, they are too hot for you to touch. The old Hispanic guy never used gloves, never gave any indication at all that the dishes were hot enough to blister skin. You can't find any gloves, so you use two dishtowels wrapped around your hands to stack the plates and saucers and coffee cups on the wire shelf, and sort the silverware into spoons, forks, butter knives, and steak knives.

Every once in a while, if he feels like he can walk away from the grill for a minute, Frank will come over and help you stack the hot dishes. He doesn't use gloves and the heat doesn't burn his skin. He doesn't say anything, and you don't acknowledge the help because you think Frank likes it better that way.

The bus pans are stacked like a wall around you. There is no way you'll ever catch up. They'll start running out of clean dishes pretty soon and Mr. Trapnell will be pissed. You decide to stop and rest a minute.

Through a crack in the wall of bus pans, you can see Frank manning the grill. Next to him is Sid, the assistant cook. Sid is an asshole. His job consists mainly of handling the deep fryers. French fries, chicken nuggets, bite-size shrimp, chicken fried steak. Stuff like that. Mostly fries. When orders are piling up, Sid talks to himself, gives himself instructions. He refers to a serving of fries as a "hit" of fries. He'll say, "We need seven hits of fries" to tell himself how many handfuls of frozen potato slices to throw into the hot oil. Anything more than ten hits of fries, Sid refers to as "boo-hoos." He'll tell himself, "All right we need boo-hoos of fries," or, when really pressed, "We need boo-hoos and boo-hoos of fries."

And sometimes you just want to scream at him, "It's *beaucoup*, you jackass," but you never do.

Frank keeps a lit cigarette on the floor at his feet, and every once in a while he will reach down and pick it up and take a secret drag. The rumbling, cavernous hood of the exhaust fan above the stainless steel grill block carries all the smoke away. It's quite a setup, and you admire it. But Frank forgets himself and lets the cigarette dangle from his lips while he works the four T-bone steaks, three patty melts, and two western omelettes he's got going on the massive steel cube.

Mr. Trapnell walks into the kitchen and sees the cigarette in Frank's mouth. The rings of fat at the back of Trapnell's neck are like a coiled garden hose that stays perpetually pink. But now that tubular flesh is bright, angry red.

"Dobbs! I told you that if I ever catch you smoking in my kitchen again you're fired. Put it out."

Frank looks up and nods his understanding. He drops the cigarette on the red clay tile floor, and squashes it under his artificial leg. Mr. Trapnell might indeed fire Frank, but it won't be right now, not at the height of the Friday night dinner rush.

One of the waitresses, Belinda, her hair permed into tiny curls wound so close it looks like they are pulling her face tight, walks in and says, "Mr. Trapnell, there's a woman out here who wants to talk to you. Says her Reuben tasted like cigarette ashes." She flicks her eyes at Frank, and you can hear a distinct note of delight in her voice.

"Shit. All right."

When Mr. Trapnell is gone, you decide to extend your break a little further. You keep watching Frank—who has already lit a fresh Marlboro. You don't see Sid though, and when you hear his petulant voice, you realize it's because Sid is now standing right beside you.

"Hey, Billy, you got that five dollars you owe me?"

You don't answer. You've been down this road

before. Sid is an asshole, but you're scared of him. You're scared of most people.

"Are you gonna pay me back or not?"

The first time he pulled this on you, you played along even though you knew it was just a con, just passive-aggressive intimidation. An unspoken threat. An unspoken threat that makes its presence felt even stronger now.

"I don't play around when it comes to money."

You speak up. "I don't owe you any money, Sid." In Sid's hair, you can see tiny grease clots deposited there by fryer fumes. They sparkle like diamonds on a turd tiara.

"Listen, you little shit, I want my money and I want it now."

"C'mon Sid, you know I don't owe you any money."

"Maybe it fell down the sink," Sid says and grabs your pale bony wrist. He escorts you—*escorts* is a good word for it—to the stainless steel sink that is as big as a bathtub. The drain is clotted with soggy scraps of food, and Sid guides—*guides* is another good word, because you're not really resisting—your hand into the drain, through the soggy slop, penetrating it, until your hand comes to an abrupt stop as your fingers meet the chunky metal teeth of the seven-and-a-half horsepower InSink-Erator, an industrial-grade garbage disposal that will virtually liquefy anything you throw in it—fruit rinds, coffee grounds, corn cobs, chicken bones. Human fingers. Really, just about anything. It's top of the line. For real, this baby is the Cadillac of garbage disposals. The stationary and rotating shredding elements are made from cast nickel chrome alloy. And the grinding chamber isolates sound and eliminates vibration. So no one will hear your fingers as they're chewed up.

"Feel around in there real good," Sid says. "Might be some money. Boo-hoos of it." Meanwhile, Sid's other hand has crept up the wall over the sink. His forefinger flips back the plastic safety dome that covers the switch that activates the disposal. The clear dome is labeled with three words: CAUTION. DANGER. DISPOSAL.

"Let me flip this light switch so you can see in there better," Sid says. His fingers play over the switch in jerky unpredictable motions. "Think it's stuck. Let me try harder."

You want to scream. A scream seems like the only appropriate response in such a situation. You're fighting now. Trying to pull your arm free. You know that Sid doesn't really intend to grind your fingers into hamburger meat. Sid is a petulant bully, but he's not crazy. At the same time, you know that this is a prime scenario for something to go completely-fucked-up-oh-my-God-somebody-call-911 wrong. And you're the one with your fingers laced around those cast nickel chrome alloy teeth with seven-and-a-half horsepower of chewing energy backing them up.

Meanwhile, the kitchen is maddeningly alive all around you. This whole thing from *Where's my money* to *Meet the disposal* has taken less than thirty seconds. Your whole life changed in less time than it takes to show a commercial on TV. Waitresses are in and out, orders are yelled, plates go up on the pass-through, and you are hidden behind all these bus pans and nobody knows that Billy Smith will probably be known as *Hook* or *Lefty* for the rest of his life. And you realize that if you end up with a prosthetic hand, that will make you more like Frank, and a certain serenity follows that thought.

"Sure you don't feel any money down there? You're playing with the devil."

And then there is a fat red blur. You will realize later that the fat red blur was a thirty-pound fire extinguisher coming down on Sid's outstretched arm. Of course what you will never forget for the rest of your life is not the sound of Sid's radius and ulna snapping simultaneously. It's not even the sight of the compound fracture poking through the flesh of the forearm. No. What you will always remember is the oddly spiritual pitch of Sid's scream. Not the scream from when his arm broke, because he passed out either from the pain or the sight of the broken bones extruding through his skin. No, it was when Frank jammed Sid's ruined arm down the gaping maw of the InSinkErator and flicked the switch—that was when Sid rose to some unknown level of consciousness and the spiritual screaming started. Frank just kept pushing Sid's arm deeper and deeper into the whirring nickel chrome alloy blades, bobbing the arm, grinding it down like he was in third grade trying to sharpen a pencil. Maybe he just wanted to smooth the splintered bones down to a satisfying point. But he gave up after a while because Sid had lost consciousness again, but still, it seemed like those screams had spurred Frank on—the same way a prayer sets God into motion. Either way, when Frank dragged Sid over to the hot grill and slid his face over it—that woke Sid back up and he started giving out with those weird spiritual screams again. Boo-hoos of them.

MR. TRAPNELL

You do not need this shit. No how, no way. How could everything have gone to hell so fast? How was it possible?

You're thirty-seven years old and you manage a Shoney's. This is not what you wanted from life. Some kid's arm ground down to a nub, his face charred, your grill looking like the Shroud of Turin. Oh my dear God.

You're going to lose some weight. Slim down. Take better care of yourself. This stress could give you a heart attack.

Fucking parolees. Uh-uh. Never again.

"Sir, Mr. Trapnell, I need you to focus."

Focus. Focus. You shouldn't be standing here talking to the cops, watching the paramedics load the assistant cook into the back of their first response unit. They built some kind of little tent thing over his face so nothing could touch it. Like that kid in *Johnny Got His Gun*. Metallica sang a song about it. Was it the one with the Sandman? Da-da-da-da...Something something...Never Never Land. Was that it? Maybe James and Lars would come on down to Shoney's and whip up a little ditty about Sid.

"Sir?"

You should be winding up the shift by now. Watching the waitresses count their tips, hearing the soft whisk of Billy sweeping the dining room, the rough scrape of

Frank cleaning the griddle with a 3M Grill Brick. Dobbs. Those tattoos. Christ Almighty.

"Did Dobbs force Billy Smith to leave with him?"

Did he abduct Billy? Kidnap him? Is that what happened? What happened? What in the fuck happened? What did Belinda say? You weren't there. You never saw what went down. But you can't see Billy Smith leaving here with a violent ex-con. No way. Not in a million years. Billy's got his issues too, but he's just a kid. Scared of everything in the world.

"He pushed him," you think hear yourself saying. "Pushed Billy out the back door and we haven't seen them since."

Then another cop comes up, reading from a printout he just got from inside the police cruiser. Those things are rolling IT centers these days. You think about computers and how much they have changed the world. Virtual reality. Like dreaming. Maybe this is a dream. Or a computer program. Or a video game.

"Franklin Arthur Dobbs. Parolee. Lost his leg in a convenience store hold-up. Cashier shot him. Dobbs's accomplice fled the scene. Left him there bleeding."

"That's what friends are for. Request a BOLO."

A video game. That's it. Dobbs looks like something out of *Grand Theft Auto*. Too violent for children to be exposed to. You knew you should never have hired him. Those fucking tattoos. But such a nice tax break. And now you're scraping some kid's face off the grill. Cleaning bone fragments out of the sink.

You haven't had a beer in three weeks. Trying to clean up your act before your heart explodes or your

liver caves in. Need to lose some weight. But you're stopping to get some beer tonight. You by God are. Fucking faceburgers.
Exit light. Enter night.

BILLY

This is why you think you've always been with Frank. Even when he wasn't there. Even before you knew him. He has always been there with you.

Frank's car is a 1997 Oldsmobile Cutlass Supreme. It looks like it used to be purple or red or something, but now it's faded and the paint has come off in big graywhite splotches like that disease Michael Jackson said he had. Vitiligo.

It feels good in the car. Quiet. The lights on Cobb Parkway make you feel warm, insulated.

You and Frank are going to Canada.

You tell him what turns to make until the Cutlass pulls into your driveway. The house is mostly dark, but you can see the faint flicker of the TV. Frank waits in the car.

You go in as quiet as you can. Grab some empty Kroger bags from under the kitchen sink.

Harvey is asleep in his chair. Passed out. You creep past him.

In your bedroom, you stuff the plastic bags with a couple pairs of jeans, T-shirts, socks, and underwear. You get your toothbrush and comb from the bathroom. Then you go back and get your Good News! razor. You don't have to shave very often, but every third week or so you start to look a little bit like a peach.

In your top dresser drawer is a photograph of your

mother. She made the frame herself. You don't have a picture of your father. Those all kind of disappeared when Harvey married your mother. Every picture that included your father just sort of evaporated so slowly that they were all gone before you realized it had happened. Your mother said Harvey was sensitive about being a replacement.

You wonder if you are starting to look like your father.

You look at your mother's picture and you feel angry at her for allowing your father's memory to be painted black. And then you are angry at her for dying, for abandoning you. But then the anger passes. Because you are older now. And you understand that maybe Harvey tricked your mother. That he hid his true self from her. That she wanted a father for you and a husband for herself. She did not know that the man she chose was only pretending that he could be those things.

And that she did not choose to die. She did not will the cells in her brain to multiply out of control. To divide into a malignant chaos. She did not choose that. Something chose that for her. She was handed that and told to deal with it.

And a cramp hits your stomach. A tiny one that focuses all its pain in one pinpoint, the way a magnifying glass focuses sunlight. And you run down to the bathroom and wad up a ball of toilet paper and put the lighter to it. You watch it burn and that pinpoint of pain diffuses as the paper burns. And when it finishes burning, that concentrated pain has washed over your entire body and morphed into a generalized discomfort that is entirely tolerable. You feel normal. You drop the last bit of the burning paper, timing it just right, so that it burns itself out as it falls, and flush it away. Normally you never burn in the house, because if Harvey ever smelled even a hint of smoke he would beat you. But you are leaving tonight, so screw him. You need the release.

You smile and grab a discarded cardboard toilet paper tube from behind the commode. You light it up. It is a pleasure to burn. You tilt the cylinder, guiding the flame, encouraging it where to feed, until the bottom rim is on fire in a beautiful circle of yellow flame. It is lovely. And the way you feel goes from just tolerable to pretty damn good. What you now feel (you know this from researching the disease with which you are afflicted), what washes over you, is euphoria. A drug high. Your glands are secreting serotonins that are pushing all kinds of wonderful buttons in your brain. You look down and the front of your pants is bulging out. And goddamn this feels good, but you can't stop to do anything about it right now. Frank is waiting. You have to hurry. You should never have stopped to indulge yourself in this second fire. You have to hurry.

You turn the burning tube upside down, hoping to get it to quickly burn itself out, down to char and ash, but the most amazing thing happens. Turning the burning cylinder upside down creates the most beautiful chimney effect. The flames, now on the bottom, race up the inside of the tube so furiously that it alarms you and immediately burns your fingers. It is too beautiful to drop in the toilet, so you set the burning tube over the sink drain. And the beauty of it is so staggering that you forget to breathe. A column of flame. Three feet high. And then it has burned itself out. The glowing ember left behind remains in a cylindrical shape and it belches a column of white smoke. Far, far too much smoke. This is bad. You scoop the ash tube and drop it in the toilet. You watch with sweet regret as it lands in the water and sizzles and extinguishes and then sinks like a crippled ocean liner.

And you realize you came in your pants. A big load. It was a pleasure to burn.

You know from past experience that if you don't stop and clean yourself up that it will dry into a protein glue that will clot the two little patches of pubic hair that you have and dry into a tight scab that will pull and pinch. But there is no time to clean yourself. You have to move. Frank is waiting.

You feel ashamed. But it felt good. Maybe the best ever. There is a haze of sharp white smoke in the bathroom, but you no longer have to worry about Harvey. You want him to smell this. To know that you were here. To smell this smoke and realize that he is smelling the real you. The real Billy Smith.

Back in your room, you pick up your mother's picture again. You can't look her in the eyes after what you just did, so instead you look at the frame, running your stinging burning fingers over it like a psychic trying to divine a message. Because she made the frame herself. There is something of her in it. She was big into home crafts for a while. Always doing things with felt and hot glue and glitter. You're about to slip the picture between the rolled-up jeans when you hear Harvey's voice behind you.

"I smell smoke."

You freeze.

"I told you what would happen if I caught you burning in the house again. Like I told that doctor. You don't need pills. You need your ass whipped."

He unbuckles his belt while he looks at you. Then he sees the bags. The photograph. "What the fuck do you think you're doing?"

Harvey staggers up to you, into the light cast by the bare hundred-watt bulb in the ceiling over your bed. The light used to be covered by a square opaque white glass fixture, but it got broke during one your fights with Harvey.

"I said what the fuck do you think you're doing?"

"I'm leaving for a while."

"You're what?"

"Moving out."

"The fuck."

"I mean, we haven't been getting along."

Shockingly, Harvey nods. Then he says, "That picture belongs to me."

"It's the only picture I have of her."

"No, it's mine," and he snatches the picture away from you.

And both of you are surprised when you snatch the photo right back out of his hands.

"Please, Harvey. This time, this one time, let me win. Let me go."

"I don't give a damn whether you go or not, but the picture belongs to me. Everything in this house belongs to me."

Harvey holds his hand out and waits for you to comply. To obey. To submit.

And the moment stretches out and you decide that

47

you will not comply. You will not obey. You will not submit.

You bolt. You feint left and as Harvey lunges to grab you, you pivot to pass him on the right. And you think you're free. But not quite yet. His meaty hand catches the back of your shirt collar and reels you back into the room.

He delivers a solid backhand blow across your face and you feel your nose pop like the skin of a fruit that is too ripe. Blood flows.

Harvey grabs the photo. If that is all he wants, then give it to him. Give it to him and get out of here. Get yourself free. Get your soul free. But Harvey has put his thick hand around your throat just under your jaw. He squeezes and lifts and he is picking you up one-handed by your neck. He pins you against the wall. With your windpipe pinched shut and your blood flow cut off you feel your face turning red and probably purple. And Harvey keeps his eyes locked on your eyes. And as you drain away, you receive the message those eyes are sending.

Comply.

Obey.

Submit.

And just before you pass out, he releases his grip. You fall to the floor and gasp for air. Feel the blood squirt through your carotid feeding your brain. Fresh red oxygenated blood spurts from your nose. The smoke from the bathroom has made its way to the air in here and traces of it burn the back of your throat.

"Leave now. Or die now."

You struggle to your feet. You leave.

FRANK

You thought you had finally licked the violence thing. But it's back. You don't feel it. You know other people feel it. Have emotions about it. But you don't feel it. You just do it. You don't get pleasure from it, though. It just pops into your mind to grind up Sid's arm like you're sharpening a pencil and you do it. Lack of impulse control is what they called it in prison. Explosive Personality Disorder. Something.

You pop the glove box and grab the package of Bronkaid you stashed in there. You had to drive to seven pharmacies before you found one that would sell it to you without a driver's license. Fucking pharmacists think they're something special. They're just pill counters. Bronkaid has 25mg of ephedrine sulfate per pill. Primatene only has 12.5mg of ephedrine, and it's ephedrine *hydrochloride*—harder for your body to absorb. You bust out four of the Bronkaid tabs, pushing them through the foil blister pack and into a bandanna. You fold the bandanna into a pouch so that the pills are in a little pocket. You crush the pills. You have to use your lighter to get them broke up, using it like a hammer, pounding the pills against the dash, then rolling it and working it like one of those crushing things pharmacists used in the olden days. Mortar and pestle. You could have been a doctor or something you bet. You like helping people. You unfold the bandanna and you have a nice mound of white powder in there. Up in Hays they called it riding the Bronk. You scoop the powder onto your thumbnail and snort it. Three snorts per nostril and it's all gone. Burns like a motherfucker. Like battery acid or something. It'll hit you in a minute. Sometimes up in Hays, a cook would be able to get the right chemicals and mix up a batch in the sink and turn this shit into crank. You could really focus then. You felt like it helped with the violence thing too. But not always. You were still prone to outbursts. They transferred you to Reidsville. That was not a promotion. On the Internet it said Reidsville housed the most recalcitrant and aggressive male adult offenders incarcerated in the Georgia Prison System. You don't know what the fuck *recalcitrant* means, but you by God understand *aggressive*. You took classes there. *Positive Mental Attitude. Anger Management. Confronting Self Concepts. Corrective Thinking.* Stuff like that. You never did shake the violence thing, though. Maybe it's the music. Maybe you listen to too much Slayer and Eyehategod and stuff, but you love death metal. Thrash. That Swedish stuff is killer. You really like that group Mayhem. You remember they got into trouble about some kind of ritual murder or something. Satanism. You wish you could kick back and ride the Bronk and chill out to some Cannibal Corpse. Even if you had some, maybe that is not the kind of music you should be exposing Billy to. He's just a kid. Still innocent. *Where is he?* You wish he would hurry up. Police could be on their way here to his house. Not cool. And no, you really shouldn't expose him to thrash metal. You would like to listen to some kind of music, though. This Cutlass you took only has an AM radio and a tape deck. You saw some cassettes in the glove compartment so you dig through them. Carole King. Joni Mitchell. Leo Sayer. Fuck. You put in the Joni Mitchell because it's got a song called "Woodstock" and you wonder if that is the Crosby Stills & Nash song. That was pretty mellow. Hippie shit. Hippies could rock back in the day. Steppenwolf. Heavy metal thunder. Fire every motherfucking gun you got and explode right the fuck into outer space. Shit like that. And you can imagine yourself out there in space. With the stars. Stars everywhere. Just surrounded by stars and rocking the fuck out. You fast-forward to the Woodstock song. Track eleven. It starts to play, and holy fucking shit, yes, it is mellow. It is far, far too mellow. It feels like a funeral in your brain, like church music or something. Just exactly like the shit that doped-up lady organist played at the church your old man dragged you to every Sunday and then beat your ass when he got you back home while your mom read Bible passages to scare the demons out of you. The spooky druggie organ music lets up after a minute and the Mitchell chick starts singing and her voice is just so squeaky like a little rat, like Mickey Mouse singing for a bunch of old women sitting in pews. We are stardust, she says, golden. And you can't believe you are sitting here listening to this hippie trippy crap. Golden? No fuck, no we are not golden. We are not golden. We are not stardust. It's just crap. Billion-year-old carbon she says, that's what we are. And it seems like this song has been playing for a billion years and fuck this noise, you just can't handle it. This is ruining your high. It puts your nerves on edge. You eject the tape and throw that shit out the window. You turn on the AM receiver. Talk radio. Neal Boortz. What a jackass. That will do.

The kid has been in there too long. At the very least the cops will send a patrol car by the house to make sure he made it home safe. To get his statement. Or maybe they would just call and talk to the father. Ask him to bring the kid to the station.

You don't want to examine why you did what you did. It is right there for you to see. Inside of you. The violence thing. The root of it. But you have to go in to get it and you don't want to do that. You did what you did.

It's pretty fucking simple. You like Billy. He reminds you of you. The kid that you used to be for maybe two seconds. Scared of every goddamn thing in the world. But then you toughened up and the world was scared of you.

And being around this kid has awakened something in you. Something dangerous. You want to find every ugly hateful thing in this world and destroy it before it destroys him. That is what you feel.

You are the kid and the kid is you. And maybe if you can protect him, if you can keep the world from having its way with him—you can see what you could have been.

And all of that somehow went through your mind when you decided to fuck Sid up. To give him something he can't take back.

Somehow, in that split second, you decided that if you save the kid you save yourself.

And then Billy is back in the car with you and you look at the blood drying in snotty scabs under his nose and you ask him where is his stuff.

"Harvey won't let—"

"I'll talk to him."

And you get out of the car and walk into the house. You decide to not think. Just do what needs to be done. You are riding the motherfucking Bronk.

The TV is on in the living room, but nobody is watching it. You can hear snoring. Drunk slobbery snoring. You head to the back of the house and find the kid's bedroom. It's a mess. Not really anything in there that would make you think it was a teenage boy's room. No posters. No baseball glove. No video games. But there is a picture on the floor in a broken frame. You pick it up and look at the photograph of the woman. You look in her eyes for a long time and then put the picture on the bed.

You go into the other bedroom where you heard snoring, and you look at the man passed out on the bed. You have decided to not think. Just do what you want to do. Let the Bronk take you where it will.

There is a cigarette burning in the ashtray next to the bed, so the guy just now passed out or is faking. You see that he smokes Marlboro Lights and that's your brand so you pocket the pack.

You lean over the guy and spit in his face. He wakes up. You pivot a little bit, balancing on your plastic leg, lifting your other leg high, rocking back to bring the heel of your boot squarely down on the guy's face. He screams. His hands go to his mouth and nose, feeling the damage. He inspects the blood on his fingers.

"Why?" The broken mouth can't actually form the word, but you know that's what he's saying.

"Because children are God's gift to us." You speak the words that were spoken to you by another man, and you cannot believe those words crossed your lips.

The guy scrambles across the mattress to the bedside table. He yanks open the drawer and pulls out what looks to be a .44 Magnum. It's certainly big enough. The bore wants to swallow you.

You look the guy in the eyes and you shrug. This confuses him, and you are pivoting again to give him a boot to the temple when he pulls the trigger and the revolver goes off like the cannon it is. The door frame behind you just fucking explodes and sharp pinewood splinters sting going into the back of your neck, penetrating so deep that they will still be working their way out of your flesh when you die a violent death—your limbs torn from your body—exactly one month from today.

You rush the guy, drag him from the bed, and take the gun away. You throw the .44 across the room. You don't want it. You don't like guns.

You pull the guy to his feet and punch him in his already shattered nose. He screams again but it's pretty muffled because of the fragmented bone and warped cartilage and the blood coating his vocal cords. It's just a kind of deep wet sound. Like pulling your boot out of sucking mud.

Then you give him one in the stomach. Not as hard as you can. Not nearly as hard as you can, but hard enough. He is completely in your control now. You ease him down back onto the bed and grab his right hand around the wrist. You extend the hand so that both of you can see it, like it was something interesting you found at a garage sale and you were showing it to him.

"Is this the one?" you ask.

The guy is not really capable of speech right now, but you pretend you don't know that.

"Is this the one?" Your voice is still calm, but there is something underneath.

The guy shakes his head. He heard that thing in your voice, that something underneath, and wants to avoid it.

"Is this the one?" And this time you roar it. Spit flies from your mouth. Years of pent-up rage.

The guy nods his head. Like a dumb animal. No, like a scared first-grader.

"I thought so," you say and you stroke the hand as if it's a woman's tit. "I thought this might be the hand you raised against a child."

You break each of the fingers on that hand. Slowly, deliberately, the way a little girl plays *he loves me, he loves me not* with daisy petals. You break them one at a time, at the knuckle. Bones crunch. Tendons pop. Pain squirts. Each broken finger punctuated by one of those deep wet bootsucking sounds you know are screams. And when you're done, the guy's hand looks like a cow's udder, the fingerteats pointing every which way.

The guy has fainted from the pain. You look at him lying there in the bed, and you see that the ashtray was jarred in the struggle and the burning cigarette has ended up in the folds of the blanket. Of course, they make cigarettes different now. They go out on their own if you don't puff on them every few seconds. You always have to relight them. Cuts down on house fires. People falling asleep smoking in bed.

You retrieve the cigarette and light that fucker up.

You hotbox it until the cherry is a long fat glowing coal and you throw it into the blankets. And you lean down and blow on it like a boy scout in the rain, like Jack fucking London, yeah, you read that story, and you keep at it and keep at it, blowing on it until the blanket material darkens and wisps of smoke curl up and you keep at it and keep at it until a lick of flame pops up and you coax it just a little more to make sure it's took hold good.

You go back to the kid's room and get his clothes and the picture of the woman who is probably his mother. And you stop a minute to look into her eyes again because you are not thinking. You are doing. And what you do is put the picture back down. You leave it. Sometimes you have to do what you are told. Sometimes you have to listen to the Bronk.

On your way out you look into the burning room and the whole goddamn bed is blazing with poisonous black smoke rolling through the top of the doorframe. And you listen a minute for the deep wet sound but you don't hear it anymore and finally the heat is too much for you and you leave.

BILLY

Frank gets back in the car and hands you your stuff. He smells like smoke. He smells good.

"What did Harvey say?"

Frank reverses out of the driveway, shrugs, and says, "The man just won't listen to reason."

"He's not a nice guy."

"Trust me, he'll burn for it," is what Frank says, and it sounds like something Arnold Schwarzenegger would say, like "I'll be back" or "Hasta la vista, baby" in one of those movies from the '80s.

"Amen," you say and the car is speeding away and you can see the house in the side mirror. See the flames raving inside.

And yes, it's true, you've always been with Frank.

Frank says he has a friend who lives in the North Georgia Mountains. Stockmar County. About two hours north of Atlanta. But you can't go straight there. Frank says you can't approach Chandler in the middle of the night. Too dangerous. No telling what his frame of mind might be. He gets paranoid. He's into that bathtub speed, Frank says.

That is what you are doing, driving around the mountains until it is light enough to approach Frank's paranoid friend. You need a place to stay, and neither of you has any money. You will need money to get to Canada. Frank's car could never make it that far, so you guys would have to save up for bus tickets. Or a train. You will need to get jobs, but probably not at Shoney's. Ha-ha. *Hasta la vista, baby. I won't be back.*

Frank listens to the radio. He doesn't listen to music. Frank likes the news. Your dad always listened to talk radio, too. He liked to listen to Paul Harvey, and you liked listening to Paul Harvey with him. You liked how Paul Harvey would tell stories, describing people so that you could see them in your mind like a little movie. And you can remember in particular one story Paul Harvey told about a kid growing up in a little small town on a mountain somewhere and how the kid liked to go fishing at this lake and how he had an old tire tied to a rope in a sycamore tree and the kid would just kick back in the tire swing and take it easy all day. Enjoying the good life. The simple life. The kid even played the harmonica. But at the end of the summer, the leaves in the sycamore turned brown, and the maple trees "exploded in crimson and yellow flames," and the kid had to go back to school. And the rest of the story was that the kid grew up and moved to Hollywood and he was really Andy Griffith and he invented Mayberry and *The Andy Griffith Show*. In real life, though, "the rest of the story" would have been that at the end of the summer when the trees exploded in crimson and yellow flames and the kid went back to school, he and a bunch of his friends stormed the school with the weapons and IEDs that they had amassed over the summer, and they killed about a hundred students and teachers before taking their own lives, and the police and media would spend years analyzing the journals, online videos, social media rants, and blog posts they had left behind and why hadn't anybody recognized that those boys were troubled and who was to blame, was it the families or was it society?

Now that would have been one hell of a "rest of the story," but Paul Harvey didn't tell stories like that and your dad is dead now and so is Paul Harvey. And that's the rest of the story.

The newscaster today isn't telling about kids who play harmonica and fish in a lake. He is talking about climate change and global warming and how parts of the planet are disappearing due to rising seawaters and everything is melting and catastrophic floods and droughts and famine and new diseases are all heading our way and there is nothing we can do to stop it. But you don't care. You just want to get to Canada before it melts and washes away. You want to see Glacier National Park. And then they are interviewing some scientist from the United Nations Weather Agency, and he says that the ozone hole over the Antarctic is one-and-a-half times bigger than it has ever been before. The ozone hole is bigger than the entire United States of America, and the radiation coming through it is giving people skin cancer, cataracts, environmental illness, and immunodeficiency, and causing animals to go blind.

All of this just washes over you in a numb sort of way because there is nothing you can do to impact it. What is there for you to do? You think about all the times you didn't put your Coke cans in the recycle bin and you wonder if a little piece of that ozone hole has your name on it. And then the scientist says that if the hole keeps getting bigger—and there is every indication that it absolutely will keep getting bigger—no one knows for sure what the result will be. And even the Arctic is losing twelve percent of its ozone every year, and over southern Canada the ozone layer is depleting at a steady rate of seven percent. And you say a silent prayer that Canada holds on. That it stays green and cold and safe.

And then the newscaster is saying how nuclear testing by the Koreans has caused a crack in the ocean floor and crude oil is gushing from it, thousands of gallons every second—*every second*—and nobody knows how to plug up the crack and thousands and thousands of gallons every second just gushing out and it could poison the whole ocean. The food chain will be devastated. People will starve.

You take your brochures out of your back pocket. They are really getting worn now. Hard to see in the dark, but there is some moonlight so you can see the pictures a little bit. You know them by heart anyway. Moonlight. You look out the window and there it is. Following you. Like it never stopped. And you look to your left and there is Frank driving, bathed in the pale green light of the dashboard instrument panel just like your father coming home from Gatlinburg all those years ago. And you feel good.

With your brochures in your lap and with Frank and the moon on either side of you, you fall asleep.

The sky is light when you wake up. The moon has deserted you. You are on a country road. No, not even a road. A path. A rutted, weeded path, and the car's worn-out shock absorbers can't keep up with the dips and bumps. This is what wakes you.

You look over at Frank. He's smoking a cigarette. He looks tired.

The car lurches through three deep depressions in the earth, rounds a curve, and there is a clearing in the trees and thick underbrush. And there is a relic of a mobile home set up on cinderblocks in the clearing. Aluminum steps. Gas generator. Propane tank. Doublewide.

Frank cuts the engine and gets out. He walks up the three creaky steps and knocks on the door. You don't think anybody is going to open it, but after a long time and a lot more knocking, you see movement at one of the windows. A corner of a sheet hanging in the window flutters. And then someone opens the door.

It is an old man. Not old-old, not elderly, but an adult. Not young like you and Frank. You are eighteen. Frank is probably in his late twenties. This guy is fifty, fifty-five. Fat. Fat fat fat. Jerry Springer fat. Doughy white. Blond hair, pale blue eyes. He's dressed all in black. Like he took a black pup tent and draped it around himself. A muumuu, you realize. It's called a muumuu. He looks like a slug. A snail peering out of its dark shell. A weak thing. But you can see enough of his eyes to know this man isn't weak.

BILLY

The man—Chandler, his name is Chandler—holds the mirror out to you, but you shake your head no. He shrugs and offers it to Frank. Frank takes it and uses the tube from a ballpoint pen to suck a line of coarse white *coke, meth, crank, what is it?* up his nose. Then Chandler takes his turn. Then they split the third line which was meant for you.

Chandler barks three times like one of those little Chihuahua dogs and then stretches his hands over his head. "My, my, my! That is sooo much better than coffee."

He works a plump finger over the mirror, collecting every last bit of residue, then swabs his gums with the finger.

"I only started with this stuff because I wanted to drop a few pounds. Slim down a little bit. It's not working."

He claps his hand down on Frank's knee—his real knee—and says, "So Frankie, I take it you two boys are in a spot of trouble." Then Chandler winks at you and says, "My boys never visit me unless they're in trouble." Then the twinkle is gone from his eye and he says, "You haven't gotten my Frankie in trouble have you?" And he is serious and you must answer him.

"No, Sir."

"You don't know what trouble is."

He lights a cigarette. It's a long skinny dark brown cigarette. Longer than any cigarette you've ever seen before. He takes his time and spews a little white cloud of smoke into the room, and then he giggles and once again Chandler is all winks and smiles. "'Sir.' I like that. Oh, Frankie, he is a taste-treat. A taste-treat!"

"Can we stay here a little while? A few days. Then we'll move on."

"What's your rush? Thought you were on parole. Thought you jailbird types weren't supposed to engage in extensive traveling."

"We just need—"

"No pigs. No pigs around here. I smell bacon, I'll turn you in myself. I have my children to protect. You know that."

He turns and gives you a wink, reaches down and pulls a photo album out from under the couch and puts it in your lap, careful of his cigarette.

"Wanna see my children? Might be you see one you recognize."

And you open the album. It's the kind with a filmy sheet of clear plastic that covers each page and you peel it back to put the photograph under it. But the pages are lumpy and have air bubbles trapped under the plastic because the photographs are all Polaroid instant film prints—the old self-developing peel-apart kind, too thick for this kind of photo book.

Chandler reaches over and flips the binder over. "Here, start at the end and go backward. It'll be like a little trip through time."

And you know right away that these are not really Chandler's children. For one thing, there are black kids and white kids and Hispanic kids and Asian kids. Nobody looks related. Almost all of them are boys, but you see one or two girls, too. And for the most part the kids look happy. They have been caught in moments of relaxation and even genuine joy. One or two have guarded expressions, as though they don't quite trust the photographer one hundred percent, but they almost do. Almost. And one boy, a little blond kid with a spiky cowlick and maybe ten years old, that boy looks scared. And his eyes are glassy and red like he just got finished crying.

You keep flipping the pages and the way the kids are dressed subtly changes. Styles from years gone by. Longer hair cropped close on the sides. Nineties styles. And you stop at a boy who's about twelve years old. His big open grin reveals a substantial set of braces. Black hair flops across a fair forehead. The dark eyes are so open, so trusting. This boy feels safe. He feels loved.

And it is Frank. The boy is Frank.

You look up at Frank, seeking confirmation, but he looks away. He does not want you to look into his eyes. Not now.

"Yep, you found old Frankie. You're sharp." And the album is whisked out of your lap and secreted back under the couch.

And part of you understands that somewhere in this trailer—or maybe buried in the backyard, or maybe in a safe deposit box—is another photograph album. A counterpart to this one. And the kids in that album don't look happy. Not at all. No, the kids in that album look more like the blond boy who just finished crying.

BILLY

The bright sunlight coming in through rips in the tattered shades wakes you up. Frank had fixed you a pallet out of thrift-store blankets beside his bed, but at some point you climbed into the bed with him. You are curled around his body, protected in his warmth.

Lying in bed, you look around the room. Frank's jeans and T-shirt are discarded on the floor, draped over his black boots—one standing upright, the other overturned. Right next to them is his artificial leg. You have seen people on TV with prosthetic legs. Soldiers back from Iraq who have skinny metal shins that connect to piston-like knee joints. You've seen athletes with legs made of curved spring steel. Titanium, probably. They look cool and futuristic.

Frank's leg looks like something from the 1970s. It's made out of hard, flesh-colored plastic. Except the plastic is not really the color of human skin. It is a dirty brown, yellowed in places. It looks old. Stained. There is a canvas sheath at the top where it cups just above where Frank's knee would have been. Fasteners and straps dangle from it. The canvas is dark and soiled from sweat and skin oil.

And here you are in bed with Frank and he is asleep next to you and you very much want to reach down and touch that part of him that's missing. Your hand begins to creep. Like a cat. Like a worm. Creeping ever lower.

And in your heart you believe that if Frank wakes up and finds you touching him in that spot, there is every reason to believe that he will kill you. Your hand slides past his stomach. Past underwear that is stretched out with a morning erection. You are going to do this. Along his thigh, silky with hair. You are prepared to slide your hand lower still when you realize that there is no lower. His leg just stops. And you bring your hand back up and you are cupping it, the stub, in your palm. It is shockingly smooth. With a knotted fissure of what must be scar tissue. This is the most private part of Frank. You have touched it. You could be with Frank for the rest of your life. Spend every minute with him. Listen to every word he ever says. Hear his deathbed confessions. His morphine-fueled revelations. And you will never be as close to him as you are right now.

You walk out the back door of the trailer. The sun is hot. Chandler sits at a circular white aluminum table under the dappled shade of a ratty umbrella. A few hundred feet farther out, a mountain creek gurgles darkly.

"Nice nappy-nappy?"

You don't say anything. You wish you hadn't come out here, but it's too late to turn around and go back inside. You wish Frank would wake up.

"Go for a swim. It'll wake you up."

Chandler is dressed in a flowing purple silky robe and nothing else. As you cross in front of him you see that his legs are apart, his genitals exposed. You get the feeling that it's staged, that it's supposed to look like he doesn't realize that his pea shooter is hanging out in the wind. Only "hanging out" isn't quite the right way to put it, because Chandler's pecker is retracted up under the substantial hood of his hairy belly, nested and peeking out from coarse gingery hair like a rodent wondering if spring has arrived.

"I don't have a swim suit."

"You don't need one. We're casual 'round here." He fans his robe as if to prove the point. You look away. "'Sides, don't have running water here. If you ever want to bathe, the creek is your bathtub."

"Is that what you do?"

"Oh sweetie, I never go near the water. I'll melt. Just like the Wicked Witch of the West."

You are happy to see Frank come out of the trailer. He's wearing jeans and boots but no shirt. The black and blue tattoos crawl across his torso as well. An intricate scrollwork of pain.

"Frankie! Where did you find this child? Eighteen? I don't know who you two think you're fooling."

Frank grunts and shakes his head.

"Well, I'm just saying. He's very photogenic. A taste-treat! I have got the fever for the flavor. Indeed I do."

"Not Billy."

"No offense, but I was just being complimentary. I don't do street trade, Frank. You know that."

Frank nods.

"Line?"

Frank nods again. Chandler produces a compact and a razor blade.

"'Sides, ever since they hooked me up like Frankenstein and zapped my head with those lightning bolts, I can't do nothin' 'cept bump pussies and giggle. Shoot!"

You have walked away from them, to the stream. You venture out onto one of the smooth creek rocks that dot the surface, and hop from one stone to another, feeling the sun shining down on you.

You notice that the creek water is not clean. It runs brown and gives off a tangy chemical odor. You look down into a pool formed by a grouping of rocks. Beer cans. A doll head. Plastic wrappers. Bits of Styrofoam. And other trash floats in a frothy, polluted brown foam.

You look back and see Frank and Chandler at the table. Standing up now. And Chandler is pointing in the direction of Frank's car.

BILLY

The woods open up to a two-lane blacktop. Chandler drives and Frank rides shotgun. You sit in the backseat, like a child.

There are cow pastures and long stretches of farmland up here. Everything is green. And after a while you drive through a tiny mountain town that is set up to look like a little Bavarian village. All the stores have the word Alpine or Heidelberg or Black Forest in their name. *Haus* is popular too. *Waffle Haus. Gas Haus.* A candy store called *Hansel & Gretel.* Everything is red and beige. The roofs of all the buildings are done up in red shingles and swoop up into exaggerated points like Dr. Seuss drew them. There is a horse-drawn buggy going down the street. The horse is a Percheron. You even see a Coca-Cola machine that is made out of wood. *Coke Haus.* People on the streets wearing dirndls and lederhosen. And then before you know it, the little town is behind you. Helen, Georgia. Now leaving Helen.

Then it is trees and pastures again. Chandler turns down a side road that leads to another side road that leads to a tiny road with a sign that says PRIVATE DRIVE.

At the end of the private drive, the crowding trees disappear and the landscape opens up to a rolling expanse of lawn that is well tended, like a golf course dotted with islands of flowering foliage.

And in the middle of this green expanse is a house.

Not a mansion, but a lavish home. Not quite an estate, but it's the closest you've ever seen.

Chandler bypasses the house and pulls up to a garage shed. A brown-skinned boy zooms out the bay door on a riding mower. The garage sits right up next to the main house, connected by a breezeway. You can tell that it was meant to house cars, but it has been converted to hold landscaping equipment.

A dark-skinned man emerges from the interior and nods to Chandler. He and Frank get out of the car. The three of them retreat back inside the shadowy garage, but from where you're sitting you can see Chandler rummaging through the airy folds of his muumuu until he extracts a manila envelope and hands it to the man. You know what is in that envelope. And as they all disappear deeper inside, you know that the dark-skinned man will have another envelope for Chandler and you know what will be in that one too.

Tonight you sleep on the couch in the trailer's living room, a threadbare blanket that smells of stale farts wrapped around you. Frank must realize that you got in bed with him the other day. You don't think he realizes that you touched that private part of him, otherwise you believe there would have been violence.

Earlier, you were watching *Midnight Cowboy* on Chandler's VCR because he doesn't have cable or satellite or Netflix or Blu-ray. But he does have a TV, a VCR, and an electric generator. You found a little three-shelf pressboard cabinet next to the TV. It held mostly books. *Hop on Pop. I Can Read. The No-Cry Potty Training*

Solution. Stuff like that. But also a few Classics Illustrated. *Moby Dick. To Build a Fire* (which you have already read in the unabridged form). *Treasure Island.* On the bottom shelf were some VHS tapes. Other than *Midnight Cowboy,* all the other tapes were kid shows like *Barney* and *The Wiggles* and *The New Zoo Review.* You almost put on *The Parent Trap* because it was the most grown-up tape you could find, but then you spotted this one at the back of the bottom shelf.

You started getting real sleepy right at the end, and it was like you couldn't tell if the movie was real or not. If you were part of the movie. Like you were Jon Voight and Frank was Dustin Hoffman and you were leaving together on the bus. Escaping. But instead of going to Florida, you were going to Canada. And it looked like everything was going to work out all right except Dustin Hoffman pissed his pants and died right there on the bus and Jon Voight propped him up because he wanted Frank/Dustin/Ratso to be right there with him when he finally escaped the filthy city. You fell asleep and the VCR shut off and the steady glowing hiss of electronic snow fills the trailer. When you wake up you feel sad, like Frank really did die, and you have to remind yourself that you're mixing up the movie with a dream and with reality. But that's not what wakes you. What wakes you is the sound of Frank and Chandler coming in through the front door.

You pretend like you're still asleep. They have a boy with them. White. Nine or ten. Chandler scoots the boy toward his bedroom. He has to use a key to open the door because Chandler's bedroom door has a deadbolt lock on it. It is forbidden to you.

Once the boy is secreted inside, Chandler rummages inside his muumuu and comes out with one of the tiny glassine packets he always has. Through your squinted eyes, you can see that Chandler is not storing these drug packets in an inside pocket, rather they are tucked up under folds of body fat. Under his man boobs. He gives the speed to Frank and then disappears after the little boy.

Frank clicks off the TV and goes into the bedroom he used to share with you.

After a long while you grow sleepy again. You are right on the edge of sleep, being pulled into it when something pulls you out of it. It is a warm moist popping sound, like a ripe seed pod bursting open. The popping is followed by a high-pitched whirring sound. *Wet pop whirr.* And the sequence of sounds repeats over and over. *Wetpopwhirr. Wetpopwhirr. Wetpopwhirr.*

You get up and tiptoe to Chandler's door. *Wetpopwhirr. Wetpopwhirr.* A flash of stark white light squeezes out from under the threshold and through the jamb. *Wet pop. Flash. Whirr. Wet pop. Flash. Whirr.*

And you can hear faint childish giggles, but you can't tell if they are coming from the boy or from Chandler.

You tiptoe back to the couch and pull the stinky blanket over your head.

WetPopWhirr.

BILLY

"What? You think I'm paranoid? You don't know what paranoid is. You don't know the feds. You don't know what they're capable of. They can see you from outer space. Satellites. Are you kidding me? Please. They can pinpoint you. You don't know what they're capable of."

Chandler's voice wakes you. It is morning. He and Frank are sitting at the little spindly card table set up in the kitchen. There is a framed mirror laid out on the table. An oval mirror with a smooth white frame. The frame is plastered with decals of Barney the purple dinosaur.

Chandler uses a razor blade to cut lines of dirty white powder on the mirror's surface. *Clackclackclackclack-clackclackclackclackclack.* He nudges the mirror across the table and sings softly while Frank does his line. "I love you...You love me...We're a hap-py fam-il-y."

He pulls the mirror back, hunches over it, and sucks up his own line. His head whipsaws back and he pinches his nose shut.

"Fuck me gently with a chainsaw. Goddamn! I don't know what Uday is cutting this shit with. Drain cleaner, maybe."

Chandler dips his fingers into a purple plastic Barney mug and snuffles the moisture from his fingertips.

"Sweet child o' mine, that feels better!"

You walk into the kitchen trying to pretend that this is normal, and really, it's not that much different from living with Harvey. You open one of the cabinets and find a box of Cookies & Cream Pop Tarts. There is only one left and the foil wrapper has been torn so the delicious breakfast pastry is stale and dry.

"I'm telling you, you don't know the feds. What they're capable of. You think I'm kidding? I kid you not. I've been under surveillance before. Why do you think I got rid of the computer? When we lived in Atlanta, they had a van parked outside my apartment for three weeks. Three weeks! You remember that, Frankie? You were just a kid. Doing kid stuff. Not a care in the world. I did all the worrying. All the looking out. Had my phone tapped. You can hear it. Little clicking noises every thirty seconds. Telltale sign. Didn't get me, though. See, if you're paranoid, they can't get you. It's the ones who don't believe—*don't believe*—who get caught. Plus. Plus I've got Bessie on my side."

Chandler reaches for a kitchen drawer behind him and extracts a revolver. It's big and heavy and ugly. He points it at you.

"Bessie never lies. She is the way. My Bessie's house has many rooms. Do you hear what I'm saying to you? She is the way. She is the truth. Billy, do you know what the truth is? Bessie's truth?"

You shake your head. You are scared. The dry tasteless crumbs of Pop Tart in your mouth go even drier and you are afraid you will choke.

"Frankie, tell him. Tell him Bessie's truth."

"Death."

"Yes! Yes sirree bob! Death! Death is the truth. Death

is the way. That's why Bessie never lies. She always tells the truth."

Chandler stops aiming at you. He strokes the gun like it's a pet hamster or something.

"With a great big hug and a kiss from me to you, won't you say you love me too?"

You look over to Chandler's bedroom door. The smooth protuberance of the brass deadbolt stares at you like a dead eye. You wonder if the boy is locked in there. You still have half of the dry crumbly Pop Tart left. Maybe you should slide it under the door so the boy has something to eat.

Maybe he is not even in there. Maybe he's at home lying in his own bed, warm under a quilt his grandmother made with the smells of the bacon and eggs and pancakes his mother is cooking filling his nose.

You eat the rest of the Pop Tart yourself.

Clackclackclackclackclackclackclackclack. Chandler hunches over the mirror, his arm a blur, the razor blade chopping up and down, up and down, like a sewing machine in a third-world sweat shop. *Clackclackclack-clackclackclackclack.* And you look at the closed bedroom door and you think, *Wetpopwhirr. Wetpopwhirr. Clackclackclackclackclackclack. Wetpopwhirr. Wetpopwhirr.*

And then Chandler is sucking water off his fingertips and pacing the cramped floorspace, his black muumuu flowing like a Stevie Nicks video.

Chandler looks at you and says, "I have a friend. A customer, really. Yes, a customer. He...well he has a taste for...one of my products. Frank met him, didn't you, Frankie?"

"Yeah, seems like a real nice guy."

"He's a gardener. Runs a crew at the Lovejoy estate across the creek, outside Helen, in Stockmar County. And my friend tells me they are still hiring groundsmen for the spring and summer."

Frank speaks up. He looks you in the eye. "We thought of a plan, Billy."

"Clean-cut teenagers," Chandler continues. "Hard workers. That's what they want. Told Uday I knew of just such a young man—"

Frank still has your attention. "We thought of a way to make some money. So we can afford to leave here. Maybe go to Canada."

"Canada?"

"—graduated early. Needs a job to save some money before he goes off to college. Squeaky clean. Squeaky. Squeaky, squeaky, squeaky. And studious. Trustworthy, loyal, helpful, friendly, courteous, kind, obedient, cheerful, thrifty, brave, clean, reverent. Yes! All those things. Yes! And on top of all of that, he's a taste-treat! A real taste-treat."

Chandler puts his puffy hand on your shoulder and speaks in a solemn, father-knows-best tone, "Billy. My boy. My son. You've got a J-O-B."

And you think, *Wetpopwhirr.*

Clackclackclackclackclackclackclackclackclack.

BILLY

It's hot. It's so hot that the heavy khaki pants and work-shirt Uday gave you to wear are soaked in sweat. You are smothering. And the droning of the riding lawn-mower combined with the heat is making you sleepy. So sleepy.

There are two other boys on mowers zooming up and down over the gentle dips and rises of Mr. Lovejoy's private golf course.

You see a battered golf cart crest a hill. It's Uday, smearing his face with a dirty bandanna. You stop mow-ing and wait for him. His cart sidles up to your mower. He extracts a bottle of water from the dingy Igloo cooler secured to the back of the cart. Just like Harvey's.

"For you," he says and passes you a water bottle, blessedly cold, sweating beads of icy moisture that catch the sun like flashbulbs popping.

Uday leans his body out of the cart and extends his hand so that he can pat your knee.

"Billy. Billy, Billy. You like it here, yes?"

"Yes, sir."

"Okay, it is hot, yes? You take shirt off, but long pants."

"Okay."

"I am clear? You take off shirt, but long pants."

"I can take off my shirt, but shorts are against the rules."

79

A giant smile breaks across Uday's face. "Yes! Mrs. Lovejoy. Her rule. No shorts. Must wear long pants. You are doing good job your first day."

Uday wipes his brow with the dirty bandanna. It must be made out of raw polyester because it doesn't absorb any of the sweat, just pushes it around his face in grimy little swirls. He stares at you. You stare at him. Waiting. His smile falters.

"You take off shirt."

You don't want to take off your shirt. Your body is skinny and pale. You want to keep your body concealed.

"You take off."

Apparently it's not an option. You really don't want to. Fuck. You unbutton the top button and Uday's smile reappears. You work the rest of the buttons and Uday smiles and nods like a parent watching a child eat his vegetables. It's good for you.

Uday smears his brow. "You see Mrs. Lovejoy?"

"No, sir."

"If you see her, you say 'yes, ma'am.' Okay? 'Yes, ma'am.'"

"Okay."

You're not hot anymore. You feel cold. Exposed. You stand up and tie the workshirt around your waist.

"Good! You are good boy. How old you are?

"Eighteen."

"Really?" Incredulous, but humoring. "That's nice."

Uday motions across the rolling green expanse, to the house in the distance.

"You don't go up there. I cut, okay?"

You nod and return Uday's smile.

"You are a good boy. Eighteen."

Uday is smiling again, but you don't see it. You are looking at the house in the distance.

You sleep on the couch that night. But you are too tired and sunburned to actually sleep. The noises keep you awake. And the corresponding little flashes of light that slither out from under Chandler's closed door.

MRS. LOVEJOY

You hate yourself.

You hate yourself so fucking much. You stand here dripping from the shower, hoping one of the Latino boys will look up and see you in the window. And want you. Want your naked body. Because nobody else wants it. Darrin doesn't want it. No, Darrin Lovejoy most certainly doesn't want it. He doesn't desire it. But he wants others to believe he does.

And you cup your breasts. The breasts Darrin Lovejoy bought and paid for. Artificial. Plastic. And you let the smooth palms of your hands awaken the nipples. And you wish one of the workers would look up here and see you and want you and desire you. That the sight of your naked body would produce a physical response in them. Through the glass and through the air you would cause pupils to dilate, blood vessels to both relax and constrict, saliva to dry up, blood to race, tissue to harden.

You hate yourself. This is what you've become. A woman who is not dried up but might as well be. You are preserved. Shellacked and encased in archival Mylar. Unused. But you want to be used.

You would leave him. You tell yourself that you would leave him. Every day you tell yourself that. Several times a day. But you can't. It's not the money. The money is nice, but money is meaningless to you. That sounds like such a fucking lie, but it's true. Money is worthless. Money has no value. Money is clean and sterile and useless. What has money done for you?

It is because of Cris. You did not know that it was possible to love something so much. You love your daughter harder than Earth pulls the Moon. This is why you can never leave. This is why you are trapped. Because Darrin loves her as much as you do. If it is possible, he might even love her more. He would let you go, but he would never let you take Cris with you. And you could never live a life in which you did not see your daughter every day. You could never live a life in which you were not the person to wake her up every morning with butterfly kisses on her cheeks, tickling her so that she woke up every morning with giggles instead of grumbles. You could never live a life in which you were not the one who made her egg-in-the-hole toast with organic eggs and the special gluten-free bread. What if you got divorced and Darrin remarried, and the substitute mother forgot and used regular bread? Or used margarine instead of pasture butter? Or forgot to replace the HEPA filter in the kitchen? Or didn't make Cris's bed with anti-allergen sheets? And you could not live a life in which you were not the one to give Cris her bath at night and tilt her head back just so because even the no-more-tears shampoo burned her delicate eyes.

And the sad part was that Darrin could not live that life either. He had to have his Crisium—he never shortened it, never just called her Cris—here every day when he came home from work, when he got back from his business trips. Darrin could never tolerate coming home to a house in which his Crisium was not here waiting for him. He could not tolerate a life in which even one hug that was meant for him might be given to a substitute father. He would do anything in his power to prevent that. And Darrin Lovejoy had quite a bit of power. Money. He had money, which was the same thing as power. Money was not so meaningless after all, was it?

And so the same old thoughts spar in your head like past-their-prime boxers, no clear winner. You are stuck. Preserved and unused and stuck.

And while your thoughts are sparring in your mind, your gaze never leaves the window. And you are being watched. Not one of the strapping Latinos or Indians, or whatever the hell they are, but a white boy you've never seen before. A skinny pale boy who looks like he might break. And your first impulse is to step back from the window. Conceal your nakedness. But you don't. You hold the boy in your eyes until he averts his gaze.

Sex. Sex is power too. You'd forgotten that.

BILLY

You are getting pretty good with the mower, zipping around like the other boys. As the golf course gives way to the lawn and the house, the landscape is dotted with islands of flora. Not azaleas and tulips and irises and pansies like you remember your mother planting in beds around your house. These are exotic, strange plants and flowers that you are unfamiliar with. Some unfold from the ground like little old ladies. Pale spindly things. Others are lush and buxom like unused women. And there is a grouping of spidery stalks that erupts irregular red, orange, and yellow tendril-like petals. Like party streamers. No, like flames. They look like dancing flames. You crane your head back to keep looking at these flowers, because they look for all the world just like fire spreading through the flower bed. You don't notice that you clipped the edge of the landscape island with the mower.

And then you see her. Marching. That is the only word for it. Mrs. Lovejoy is marching across the lawn, heading straight for you. She is wearing sandals, white shorts, and a yellow tube top. Sunglasses that seem as big and round as pizza pans. The tube top exposes the tops of her breasts, warm and brown like the backs of sleeping puppies. She is waving at you, a cigarette clamped between fingers trailing white smoke. Her mouth forms words. Angry words.

You halt the mower, idling. You have no choice. She saw you. The other day. Looking at her. Spying on her through the window.

"Did you see what you just did?" she shouts at you over the rumble of the engine.

You tilt your head like a quizzical dog.

"Would you turn that thing off?"

"What?" you yell back even though you understand her.

"I said turn that—"

You cut the engine.

"—goddamn thing off," Mrs. Lovejoy yells into the now quiet day.

"Sorry," you say.

"Did you see what you just did?"

You shake your head.

"Well, the flowers you just ran over were imported from China. Extremely rare."

She drops her cigarette onto the grass, and then she is down on her hands and knees, pawing through the confetti-like mess your lawnmower has left in its wake. Mrs. Lovejoy rises to her knees, her hands cupped in front of her, her eyes angled upward to you.

"Orb of the Night. It's called Orb of the Night."

In her cupped hands is an ovoid pouch made of fleshy coral-colored petals. Like skin.

"It opens at night," she says and forces the petals back, exposing the silky red interior to the sunlight it was never meant to see.

You swallow hard. It feels like the two of you are looking at a pornographic image instead of a broken flower.

"You killed it," she says and tosses the remains to the ground like a nurse tossing out the remains of an abortion.

"I'm sorry. I'll pay for it."

Mrs. Lovejoy finds her cigarette smoldering in the grass and performs CPR on it, puffing it back to life. She stands. She is taller than you. She takes a long, final draw from the cigarette and exhales a flower-like plume of smoke. You can see the anger leaving her.

"Are you new?"

"Yes, ma'am," you say, and it occurs to you that if she saw you run over the flowers in the split second that it happened, then it was either incredibly bad luck or she has been watching you.

"'Ma'am,' Oh, I like that. And what's your name?"

"Billy."

"Billy? Well, Billy, as I was saying, that flower was extremely rare. I don't care about the golf course or the gardens, but these, all this, is mine. Do you understand?"

"Yes, ma'am, I'll be very careful from now on."

She reaches out and almost touches your bony chest. But she pulls her finger back at the last second.

"Better put your shirt back on. You're getting pink."

"Yes, ma'am," you say and watch her walk away.

BILLY

She is blond and thin and big-breasted like the girls at school who do not look at you. Except she is old. Old enough to be your mother. She is the kind of girlwoman who can choose any boyman she wants. And you are never that choice.

Throughout the rest of the day, whenever you look up to her window, she is there, looking down at you. Night comes and you are the last one here. Everybody else has gone home. It is a five-mile walk through the woods and across the creek to get back to Chandler's, but it is thirteen miles by car. You kept finding things to do to occupy you as the others left. And finally Uday left. And you are alone in the garage.

You know what you want to do. It is time.

From the garage window you look up at the house. To the window where Mrs. Lovejoy displays herself to you. She is watching you and you are watching her. Two windows and two hundred yards separate you. She is performing for you. Showing. There is a word for it when animals behave like this. *Presenting.* She is presenting herself to you. But you are not responding. Because what she is offering, what she is presenting, is not enough. You need more. You look down at yourself and no, it is not enough. You are shriveling. Mrs. Lovejoy is not enough by herself. Maybe because it isn't a secret anymore. Maybe because she is complicit. You need something more to make it work for you. Flame. You need fire. You search the shed trying to find something that you can hold in your free hand while it burns. All you can find is a pinecone on the floor. You know that the sticky pine sap will flame nicely and your erection returns in fiery anticipation.

You set the pinecone afire with your lighter and lay it at your feet. You can feel the heat warming your naked thighs, your swollen genitals. And you look back out and Mrs. Lovejoy is no longer in her window. It is just an empty rectangle of soft white light.

"Is that supposed to be a candle in the window for me?"

You are caught. Literally caught with your pants down. And a forbidden fire. In one fluid movement you pull up your pants and stomp the pinecone out under your workboot.

"I'm sorry. I'm so sorry. Don't tell."

"Don't tell who? It's just you and me." She is wearing jeans and an unbuttoned blouse, her bra visible.

"I'm sorry."

She does not respond. What she does is slip off her blouse. She reaches behind and unfastens the white bra. And her breasts swing free and they are perfect full glands. Substantial flesh that gravity has somehow not yet touched. And you realize they must be implants. That her husband bought those for her.

"If we're going to look, let's see what we're looking at. I wanna see. Do you wanna see?"

You nod your agreement and you are scared to death. You have never had a sexual experience with another human being. You do not know what to do. Your heart is beating so hard and so fast you can feel it in your throat, choking you, robbing you of air.

Mrs. Lovejoy tugs down her soft faded jeans. She is not wearing underwear. Her stomach is flat and tan and tapers down to a pale planchette of rough hair. Way more hair than you have. And in the moonlight streaming in—*yes, the moon!*—you can see tiny flecks of moisture caught in the lower part of that tangle. Little slippery beads. And she parts the planchette and presents herself to you. And you see. It is red and smooth and deep. And she spreads herself apart and it is so smooth and so red and so wet. And the entire world is red smooth wetness that promises a depth that will pull you down into it, and that is where you want to be that is where you want to go that is where you want to go that is where you want go and Jesus Jesus Jesus your pants are back around your ankles and her fingers have disappeared in the smooth red wetness first one then two then three and you do not need the fire you do not need the fire this is all you ever wanted this is all you ever wanted this is all you ever wanted. And she is crying out like she is in pain. Over and over, crying out. It is spiritual. Like Sid's pain, Mrs. Lovejoy's pain is spiritual.

Your orgasm is different, stronger, more intense. It comes from a place within you that you have never drawn from before. You do not even have to touch yourself. You take your eyes off of the red wet smooth world only long enough to look down at yourself. At the five-and-three-quarter inches of your carefully measured, mostly bald dick. It twitches like a divining rod that has sensed a massive underground lake. It spasms, again and again, bringing up thick streamers of ejaculate, not the watery seminal fluid you are used to, but gelatinous opaque semen that arcs through the air and lands at Mrs. Lovejoy's feet like an offering. Like alms.

FRANK

You are riding around with Chandler. Tweaked on crank. Or something. Whatever that powder is. Bath salts. Molly. Krokodil. Carpet cleaner. Who the fuck knows? Your mind is racing. Your thoughts are no-thoughts. You do not want to have thoughts. You want what is to come—to come. Let life wash over you. Do not let your thoughts try to alter the future. The future is set in stone. Carbon fiber. Billion-year-old carbon.

But then Billy creeps into your mind. And your no-thoughts become real-thoughts and real-thoughts are just an attempt to change a future that will not be changed. *Billy.*

Chandler speeds past a burnt-out gas station. Esso. You flip down the passenger-side visor and look at your face in the dirty mirror mounted there. You've got a pimple on your cheek. Like you're a teenager again. You set a finger on either side of it and squeeze, but it won't pop. It isn't ripe enough to pop yet. You need to stop fucking with it. It's getting red. Inflamed. Probably impurities in that bathtub speed working their way out of your body. No telling what Uday cuts it with.

The road opens up and green pasture rolls by on each side, hemmed in by rusty barbed wire. Cows grazing. After a while, Chandler pulls off to the side and stops the car. He tells you to roll down your window, so you do. It is ingrained in you. You do what Chandler tells you to do. He pulls Bessie from under the seat and leans across you.

Someone watching from a distance would see a once-red but now washed-out-burgundy 1997 Cutlass Supreme. From the passenger window of the Cutlass, an arm extends holding a handgun. The Colt SAA seems to scan the field, before taking aim at a cow in the distance. The innocuous pop of the revolver firing is later followed by the pleasant odor of burnt propellant wafting in the clean mountain air.

The bullet misses the cow but digs a divot in the earth that disturbs the bovine. The cow moves away, lumbering. What the observer then sees (and you are the observer, your no-thoughts place you outside of yourself sometimes, just an onlooker watching your own life unfold) is a profoundly fat man heaving himself up out of the driver's side of the car, the folds of his black muumuu billowing grandly like a judge or a nun. The fat man yells back into the car, "Hey Frankie! Watch this!"

The fat man crosses in front of the car to the shoulder of the road. In a feat of contortion you would not think possible for someone so large, the man holds the gun two-handed, behind his back. Then he bends over so that he is peering between his legs, under the hem of the muumuu, looking back at the now meandering cow. He aims. Technically, the fat man is shooting the revolver both behind his back and upside down. He fires. The slug pierces the animal's brain. The cow drops.

"Now that's shooting!"

It takes the fat man far longer to unbend himself and stand erect than it did for him to bend over and fire. But eventually he rights himself and squeezes his body back into the sedan. He has to pull the door two times before it pushes his fat out of the way enough to click shut.

The Cutlass takes off, as slow as the lumbering cow once was. The car looks misshapen, knocked out of true with the driver's side riding too low to the ground.

Chandler steers with his knees while he replaces the spent rounds in the revolver.

"What the fuck does he think this is? Vacation fucking Bible school? An after fucking school job?"

Chandler is different now. He didn't used to be like this. He was sweet. Kind. You know they did something to him up at the Diagnostic Prison. Hooked him up to some machine. Or maybe it was just the speed.

Chandler puts the gun back under the seat and lights up a joint sprinkled with dust. You have done so much powder you feel that the molecules of your body have become polymer. You are chemical and plastic. You are spun. You are poly. You are stardust. You are golden. You hit the joint when Chandler passes it to you. You have not slept or eaten in three days. How can Chandler be so fucking fat and tweak nonstop? How is that possible?

"He's supposed to be watching the place so we can rob it. 'Oh, they've got a really neat garden.' What the fuck is that? Bullshit! That's what the fuck it is. Who is this kid? Harry Potter? I'm telling you we've got to move. The feds. The feds. You think local cops are bad? You don't know. Do you hear what I'm saying to you? The heat. The heat is closing in. I've got to have money. You don't know. You don't know what I've seen."

You are chemical. You are synthetic. And you've got to get yourself back to the garden.

"White slave market. We could sell the kid. Young white kid like that. Two thousand. Easy. I'm not kidding. You think I'm kidding? You don't know."

You place your hand on Chandler's right knee and apply downward pressure. The Cutlass grunts and lurches forward. You use every crank-fueled sinewy synthetic bit of strength you have to force Chandler's leg down and onto the accelerator.

Chandler screams like a girl as the Cutlass flies into a mountain curve. The speed is exhilarating. It cleans your mind of the toxins trapped there. Maybe this will clear up the pizza face you're getting. You feel the molecules of your body melding with the car. You are synthetic-goldenstardustchemical.

The car is all over the road. The pasture land is gone, replaced with steep mountain passes, now just a golden chemical dropoff. Death.

Finally Chandler's screaming pierces the plastic film in which your mind has been wrapped.

"...are you doing? Are you crazy? Die! We'll die. We're gonna die! You're gonna kill us. I'm sorry! I'm sorry! I was just kidding! FRANKIE!!!! PLEASE!!!!!"

You release Chandler's leg. The Cutlass returns to normal speed. Chandler is hyperventilating. He tries to push words out of his mouth, but his lungs want air flowing in only.

"What...fuck...wrong...you...crazy?"

The spiked joint has gone out, so you fire it up. Billion-year-old carbon. You are stardust. You are angel dust. You are devil dust. You are Sevin Dust. You are house dust. You are Endust. And you've got to get yourself back to the garden and dust that motherfucker.

You put the roach between Chandler's lips and he slurps on it like a kid with the dregs of a milkshake. You wait until Chandler has got himself together. This is the first time you have ever stood up to Chandler. You look him in the eye.

"Don't ever talk about hurting Billy."

"It's cool, Frankie. It's cool. I was just kidding around. For the love of fuck. Almost killed us."

"You coulda put your other foot on the brake."

"Guess I wasn't thinking clearly. Didn't realize there was going to be an impromptu driving exam. Next time I'll study beforehand."

You flip the visor down and get back to work on that zit.

BILLY

You are fucking her. You are actually fucking her.

She grabs hold of your skinny white ass, pulling you deeper inside her. She wants every bit of that damn-near six inches of dick that juts like stone from between your legs. She wants it between her legs. And you are actually fucking her.

She brought you up to her bedroom. She took your clothes off. Stripped you. And you were afraid that you would not be hard. Because this was not jacking off. This was touching. This was touching another person and that person touching you. And she undid your pants and pushed them down to your ankles and your almost-half-a-foot of cock sprang out like a steel rod, like a lead pipe, and her mouth was on it hungry for it and she took it all the way in, her lips touching the patches of pubic hair, and up and down and up and down and she was living for it, living for it. And you were not thinking of fire. Not thinking of fire. This was normal. And she pushed you back on the bed and you were amazed at how cold and soft the sheets were and then she was pulling off your shoes and socks and tugging your jeans completely off. And your cock beat and bobbed and bounced on your belly—cold and hard as her saliva evaporated on the shaft. And you could feel it maybe shrinking a little bit. Shriveling. Getting soft. And you wished you could hold fire in your hands. A flame to excite you. But then she was on top of you and you didn't know when she took her clothes off, but they were off and she was naked, her tits like something drawn on a bathroom stall. And in a single fluid movement she was on top of you, tits swaying, her hand guiding your just-hard-enough cock inside her as she opened her red orb to you, for you and only you the red silky flesh was open and it grabbed hold of your cock and you were rock hard and thrusting up as she was thrusting down and you leaned your torso forward to catch those swaying fantasy tits in your mouth but they were too fast and too heavy and you sucked and bit at them as they swung past and your lips sometimes latched on and then lost them again.

And then she was making her own sounds. Tiny little pet sounds that were just for her but getting louder. And you could smell the funk and the musk of all the juices that were flowing through her and dripping down your balls and slicking your thighs and that smell drove you crazy. And then she was screaming. She was screaming. Not just screaming but screaming your name. *Billy.* She was screaming Billy and then she was sitting straight up on you, grinding herself brutally against her cock. No, not her cock. Your cock. Your cock your cock your cock. She ground so hard and her pussy grabbed hold so tight that it hurt you but she was finished screaming. It was over. That part was over. And she rolled off you. Except that she held onto you when she rolled. So that you were then on top of her. You never separated. You stayed plugged in. And then you started humping. Clenching your butt cheeks and sliding deeper into her. And out of her. And in. And faster. And deeper. And you are fucking her. You are actually fucking her.

You do not need fire.

You are pounding her. You are a man. You force her legs rudely apart. You grab her by the ankles and spread her legs as wide as possible and she gasps as you go ever deeper and she has no choice this is what you want and you will do whatever you want and you do not need fire and she can't stop you even if she says no more she can't stop you and you have her feet pinned behind her head and feel that cock bitch feel that cock take it take it take it and she likes that and you pound and pound and your body is a weapon you are using against her your cock is a weapon and she is powerless to stop you and spread those fucking legs bitch you are moving up and down back and forth so fast and she is so wet and so powerless against you and you are panting like a dog in the sun and crying out as fast as you are pounding and she can't ever stop you.

It is a pleasure to fuck.

DETECTIVE JERNIGAN

You have scheduled this training to coincide with your regular chat session with Madison, a girl you have never met. You want the cadets to see how easy it is to manipulate a child.

ROCKERME — So u finished it

MADISON_44 — 2nite prob

ROCKERME — ur team win the game ystrday?

MADISON_44 — bruins 11 allstars 2 wut u think

ROCKERME — think u guys kicked srius butt

MADISON_44 — LMAO!

ROCKERME — :)

MADISON_44 — how r u guys doing? Still losin?

ROCKERME — don't ask :(

"Children think they are safe. They think they are Internet savvy. And they are. Children today are raised to be suspicious and wary. For good reason. But, still, they are only children. And children can be tricked.

"I talk with Madison every day at this time. Three-thirty. Except the days she has a game. I think I can safely assume that she gets home from school at that time. And no one is there to monitor her Internet use. Her parents receive logs of their daughter's phone texts, but Madison knows how to cover her tracks online. She likes privacy.

"Now Madison would never tell a total stranger where she lives. She's too smart for that. She would never tell me the name of her school either. But I do know she walks home from it every day. She told me that. I mean, what harm could it do? It's just a bit of trivial knowledge, right? It's not like I know what school she goes to."

MADISON_44 — parent tchr conf this week
MADISON_44 — sux.
ROCKERME — ours last week. My rents didn't go
MADISON_44 — mine r going – 2nite!
ROCKERME — that kinda sux
MADISON_44 — no kidding
ROCKERME — hit me up 2mro tell me how it went
MADISON_44 — k. ttyl

"But I do know that she probably lives somewhere in metro Atlanta. We met in a local chat room. I also know that only one elementary school in the metro area has a girls' softball team called the Bruins. And I know that Madison is number forty-four on the team. In fact, I already knew that the Bruins won their last game, before Madison told me. I was there. I watched her play. And I followed Madison_44 home after the game. She didn't see me. But I saw her. In fact, I saw where she keeps the key to her house hidden. It's tucked in the dirt of a cracked flower pot on the porch.

"And now I know that Madison will be alone this evening."

You look at the small group of men and women who are watching you, and you say: "And tonight I'm going to pay Madison a visit. I'm going to her house and I'm going to get inside that house. Lucky for Madison, I'm not a monster. I'm going to wait until her parents get home. And we'll all sit down together and talk about the real monsters."

You dismiss the young recruits from the training you've just given them.

Your name is Joe Jernigan. Detective Joseph Jernigan. The words SPECIAL VICTIMS UNIT are stenciled on the door to this room that houses your desk and those of the other members of your department. The Special Victims Unit investigates rape and other sexual assaults, cases of child exploitation, child abuse, missing juveniles, and child neglect. On your desk are three framed photographs. Two photographs of your daughter, school pictures. Fourth grade and fifth grade. And one photograph of you, your wife, and your daughter. Big white smiles like a toothpaste commercial.

You have been with the Atlanta Police Department for nineteen years. Right out of the Academy you were assigned to Patrol Zone One in West Atlanta, and there you did see some shit. You worked the Bluff, Bankhead Courts, and Bowen Homes. You saw some shit, it is true. The Gangs and Guns Squad. You made Detective and served in the Central Investigations Division of the Major Crimes Section. A few years later you were promoted to Sergeant in the CID. You did well. For a while. Then two years ago you requested a demotion, a "non-lateral transfer" back to the rank of detective and reassignment to the SVU. There was resistance from above, but you had made friends in the course of your career. You called in favors. Made promises. You got what you wanted.

Your partner is standing over you. Detective Mike Burdick. He is at least fifteen years younger than you. And like every other detective in Special Victims, he sees this assignment as a stepping stone on his way to Homicide. That's generally the way it goes. Nobody wants to make a career out of sex crimes. Except you. Other officers and detectives tend to keep their distance from you. Even Burdick. He's friendly, but he keeps it strictly professional. You do too.

"I think I've got something on that kiddie porn."

"Child abuse images," you say. A gentle reminder.

"Right."

"Which do you mean? Narrow it down for me."

"Small-time stuff that's been showing up in Cabbage-town. Real young kids."

"Right. Is it someone in town? One of the local perverts?"

"Remember the guy in Vine City with all the VHS tapes and Polaroids? The old-timey stuff?"

"The one that molested three boys in his scout troop? But it was all just a misunderstanding and the parents of two of the boys even testified in the guy's defense? That guy? The one who, because of the hearing loss in his left ear, didn't understand his rights, and all those nostalgic tapes and pictures couldn't be entered into evidence? That guy?"

"'Be prepared.' Well I've had one of the patrol units grabbing the guy's trash. About once a month or so they'll take a bag from curbside and I go through it. Why not? It's legal. Anyway, three different times now

I've found padded mailers with no return address and a Stockmar County postmark."

"And?"

"And I got an up-to-date list from the GBI. Guess which of your favorite sexual predators is now registered in Stockmar County? John Chandler Norris."

"The Polaroid King. Chandler Norris is in Central State lockup."

"Well, he was. For a while. There were some 'psychiatric symptoms' that came to light in the Corrective Thinking program, and in the name of liability he was shipped up to Georgia Diagnostic and Classification Prison."

"You're shitting me. I'm guessing they didn't transfer him up there for death row."

"Not quite. He was diagnosed with depression and catatonia. Electroconvulsive therapy was administered and deemed successful."

"You are fucking kidding me. They zapped the evil right out of him. Is that what you're saying?"

"Like one of those bug lights. Zzzzzzpt."

"This world is completely fucked. So they cured him?"

"I don't know, Joe. All I know is that they released him. He registered himself with the local authorities as a sex offender and got himself set up on top of a mountain somewhere. It's all Grizzly Adams and shit."

"And you think he's running some kind of mail-order child pornography business out of Stockmar County?"

"I think it's worth a visit."

"I do too."

BILLY

The picture of the little girl freaks you out. She is there every time you fuck her mother. Right there on the bedside table, watching you slam Mrs. Lovejoy. She looks to be about seven, with blue eyes and wispy blond hair. She looks fragile. Like a flower in a vase right before the petals start to drop off. One time you were fucking Mrs. Lovejoy so hard with the headboard banging the wall and the mattress rocking the bedside table that the little girl's picture fell over and when you were done fucking her mother you propped the picture back up because you did not want the little girl to be face down in the dark.

Crisium. Her name is Crisium. You know that much only because Mrs. Lovejoy has mentioned her in passing, talking on her cell phone, making doctors' appointments, talking to her husband, arranging times to meet with you based on her obligations to Crisium. But Mrs. Lovejoy does not talk *about* Crisium. Not to you. And you have fucked her seven times now (twice on three different days and just the one time on that first day), and you still call her Mrs. Lovejoy.

She rolls off of you (Mrs. Lovejoy likes to finish on top) and starts puffing on a Nicotrol inhaler. She only smokes cigarettes outside. Never in the house. You ask her why she doesn't just open the window and smoke a real cigarette. You figure she will say her husband might smell it, but what she says surprises you.

"If I smoked in the house, it could kill Cris."

This is the first time Mrs. Lovejoy has spoken her daughter's name directly to you.

"Does she have asthma?"

Mrs. Lovejoy puffs on the stubby little nicotine inhaler.

"She's in the hospital. She has MCS."

"What's that?"

"Multiple Chemical Sensitivity. That's why we moved here, away from the city."

"To get away from chemicals?"

"She...You can't get away from chemicals. That's no longer possible in this world. Chemicals, fumes, exhausts, reagents, fertilizers, pesticides, plastics, synthetic fabrics, petroleum products, paints. Second-hand smoke. The list goes on forever. You can't escape those things. Not anymore. Not in this world. But you can lessen your exposure."

"We cut down the rainforests, and a little girl gets sick."

Mrs. Lovejoy looks at you with a peculiar expression on her face and you realize that she is trying to figure out if you are being serious or if you are making fun of her or, worse, making fun of Crisium. And her face softens as she decides that you mean exactly what you say.

"Yes!" she says, holding your eyes with hers. "That is exactly right. That is the world we have created. That is the world we are living in."

"For every action, there is an equal and opposite reaction."

"Her immune system is haywire. Some people call it Environmental Illness. It amounts to the same thing. The world makes Cris sick."

BILLY

"A little girl!" Chandler gushes like a little girl himself. "Well, friends and neighbors, that right there is a game changer."

Frank is in the kitchen. Cleaning his plastic leg with alcohol pads and Windex. He has been scrubbing and rubbing at it for two days now. Trying to get it just right.

"And she wants you to drive them to the hospital for the what-was-it treatments?" Chandler asks.

"Interferon," you say. "Mrs. Lovejoy wants to help me make more money. For my education."

"Bessie'll educate her. Rich cunt."

"It could be done," Frank says and rubs a little harder at the stubborn spot that only he can see. It just won't go away.

Frank sits there, dressed only in gray underwear— worn-out jockey shorts, the elastic shot. And the tattoos cover every inch of his body—arms, neck, sporadically to his face, even peeking out from his scalp, densely inked torso, disappearing to his groin, down his legs, between his toes—and the funny thing is that his artificial leg is the only part of him that is unblemished, still pure. And yet he thinks it's dirty. The only time you have seen Frank stop rubbing and polishing that leg is when he goes to the bathroom, and you're pretty sure that what he does in the bathroom is work on that zit on his face. There isn't much else he could be doing in there because you never see him eat or drink anything, but every time he comes out of the john, that zit is redder. Inflamed. You know he's been squeezing it, working it. And you want to tell him to maybe just use some soap and water because his face is so oily and he smells kind of bad, but you could never say something like that to Frank.

And it occurs to you that there was another Ray Bradbury book you saw in the school library. But you never read that other book. You only read *Fahrenheit 451*, over and over again. But you wish now you had read the other one, too. It was called *The Illustrated Man*. And just like Ray Bradbury had written the book about burning just for you, he had written *The Illustrated Man* just for Frank, and you wish you had read it.

"Of course it can be done," Chandler says. "We just have to wait. Bide our time. An opportunity will present itself. They always do."

"Take Cris?" you ask even though you know damn well that's what they're saying. "Frank, that's crazy."

"Boy, you don't know what crazy is. Wait'll they hook your head up to a car battery, then maybe you'll know what crazy is."

Frank says, "I thought you wanted to go to Canada."

And of course you want to go Canada where the birds sing and the snow falls in white wet whispers and you don't have to get your head hooked up to car batteries. "I do," you say.

"We have to have money," Frank says, and his tone is so reasonable. He fastens the prosthesis to his thigh,

cupping it to the fissured stump. The canvas straps are still sweat-stained and filthy. "This is the perfect way. No one will get hurt."

"All we do is hold the girl right here. For three days she watches cartoons and eats Pop Tarts. It'll be like summer camp. An adventure."

"Chandler's good with kids," Frank says.

But you look at the deadbolted door to Chandler's bedroom and you think about watching *Midnight Cowboy* and choking on stale Pop Tarts. Then you look at Frank and you've always been with Frank and he will protect Cris. You know that in your heart. Frank will protect Cris. And you will do what you have to do to get Frank and yourself to Canada.

"She said I could stay in a room over the garage until school starts back up. If I wanted."

"Your own place, huh?" Chandler asks. "That's good, boy. In fact, that's great."

"So I can save for college." *So you can fuck her whenever she wants.*

"Right," Chandler says, like he can read your mind. "Whatever. She wants in your pants. If she hasn't already got in 'em." Chandler puts his arm around you, pulls you close in a grandfatherly hug. "Cougar found herself a cub. But that's good. Just remember why you're there. And remember this. When she visits you one night—and she will—just remember, hell hath no fury like a woman denied oral gratification." Chandler cackles with glee and looks you in the eye. "You gotta eat dat tang!"

Chandler does a crazy dance around the room, a herky-jerky strut that makes the entire trailer shake. And you watch him. And it occurs to you that the hole in the ozone layer is spreading. Expanding over Canada. And you better hurry. You better hurry before it's too late. Before Canada burns up. Before the glaciers melt and black oil fills the oceans and they boil down to a toxic sludge.

FRANK

The wheels on the bus go round and round, round and round, round and round.

The sun feels good on your face and neck. Maybe the UV rays will dry up your skin a little bit.

You hold your arms out, hike up your sleeves, and look at the blue and black jailhouse tattoos that flourish there like old-man liver spots.

You hate the tattoos. The Frank that once wanted those tattoos is gone now. The tattoos were necessary once. They told the world you were not to be fucked with. The limp and the artificial leg made you a target in prison. A good choice for natural selection. Weak. It was a weakness that the strong would see and then seek you out as easy prey. So you covered yourself in prison ink. Of course you had to back it up with action. So you became an animal. A violent animal. And you changed your outside to reflect what you became inside. Ink made from urine and soot, ashes and shampoo, etched onto your body with paper clips, staples, electric toothbrushes, and guitar strings. Spider webs and ornate crosses. Album covers. Barbed wire and serpents. A crying woman and half a swastika. Your parole came through before your cellmate could finish the swastika. You are not a skinhead. Not an Aryan. Except you are because in prison you have to be a part of something bigger or that bigger something will swallow you. In prison, you submitted. And later, you made others submit.

The wheels on the bus go round and round, round and round, round and round.

You hate the tattoos. You are ready to change back. You are ready to change both your outside and your inside. Because inside you still feel like a child, and outside you look like a threat. A dangerous violent man. And of course you really are a dangerous violent man. But inside, the boy who needed protecting, the boy who needed love and safety is still alive. Barely.

The sing-song nursery rhyme lilts through the air. Chandler is playing his music on the Cutlass's tape deck. The music calms him. The music makes you sick. You can't close your ears, so you tilt your face so that you are looking directly into the sun, hoping that by concentrating on the pain in your eyes you'll no longer hear the music. You can feel the solar radiation burning your retinas. And maybe God can see your tattooed tears. Maybe He will notice.

"That, and beating off, will make you go blind, Frankie."

The Cutlass is angled onto the shoulder of the road. The hood is up, the hazard lights blinking.

The horn on the bus goes beep beep beep, beep beep beep, beep beep beep.

"I swear, I've never known you to be such a worry-wart." Chandler scans the road ahead with a dented pair of binoculars.

"I don't think I've got the heart for this kind of stuff anymore," you hear yourself saying from inside the white-hot blindness. You've closed your eyes to the sun, but it bleeds like phosphorus through your eyelids. Inked on the lids are the words *Don't Wake*. It's a Russian thing. It was once a message to other cons, now it's a message to God.

"Heart? Why, I didn't know you had a heart, Frankie."

"It's Billy, you know?" And you think, *Who is this man who speaks from the white-hot light? He is not a violent convict smeared with prison ink. Who is he? Does he really exist?*

"Know? Do I know? You don't know what caring for someone is. I know what caring is. I care for my children. I love them. I show them more love than they've ever known before. I took care of you."

"Yeah, you took care of me. And maybe I don't know what caring for someone is. But I'm learning."

"Why, I declare, Frank, I believe you've got a little sugar in your britches. 'The wipers on the bus go swish, swish, swish; swish, swish, swish; swish, swish, swish.' All this emotion. It doesn't suit you. You need a bump."

And you do. A good bump up each nostril. Plastic elastic. Billion-year-old carbon.

"Billy wants to go to Canada. Build a cabin in the woods. Me and him. Just live out there. In nature. I mean, I like that."

It is very quiet after you speak. Chandler's tape has ended. Then you hear him snicker. And giggle. He says, "And God bless Ma and Pa and little Billy and all the Waltons on Walton's Mountain and all the Whos down in Whoville and my fucking God Frank what has happened to you?"

You do another bump off your thumbnail. Chandler

rewinds his tape and once again the wheels on the bus are going round and round, round and round.

"What time is it, Frankie?"

"Skin-thirty. How the fuck should I know?"

"Well excuse the hell outta me." Chandler puts down the binoculars long enough to glance at his watch. "It's eleven-forty five. He said eleven-thirty. Maybe he decided to take the cunt and go build a little house on the prairie with *her.*"

"He'll be—"

"Okay! Okay! I think...That's them! That's the car! Get your mask. Battle stations! Battle stations!"

And a surge of adrenaline is pumped into your body by your adrenal glands. It squirts out the glands and instantly your heart beats even faster, your blood vessels constrict even tighter, but you don't feel it. You are far too tweaked to feel anything biological. You only feel synthetic. Plastic. Billion-year-old carbon. Nonetheless, the synergy of the adrenaline and the crank creates a momentary window of reason. For one brief instant, you can see unaltered reality. Your thought process returns to that of a normal, rational man. And you realize that you and Chandler have not planned this thing at all. No thought or care or consideration has gone into it. All of the gaps in logic and common sense have been filled in with crystal. With carbon. With stardust. So that on the surface it appears smooth and reasonable. And you now see what you are about to do for what it really is. Stupid. The stupid callous dangerous foolhardy act of two common criminals. Everything will go wrong. You will be caught.

But then the window of clarity slams shut and once

again irrational self-confidence floods your brain. You are a criminal mastermind. This is the perfect plan. No one will get hurt.

Once again, you are stardust.

BILLY

...Uncontrollable urges to kill and have sex with the dead bodies. Unsubstantiated reports claim that Williams preserved the heads of his victims in glass jars filled with a homemade concoction of—

Mrs. Lovejoy leans forward and switches the radio off.

"Jesus Christ, what is this world coming to? The oceans are poisoned with bubbling oil. It's like Jed Clampett shot his rifle into the sea, except this time he used a nuclear warhead, and now some crazy is killing people and preserving their heads in jars. My dear God."

"I know," you say, because you don't know what else to say. There is nothing else to say. You just look forward and drive.

"I'm glad Cris didn't hear that."

You glance in the rearview mirror and see Cris sleeping. She is pale, her eyelids a bruised peach color. When you picked her up from the hospital, they rolled her out in a little wheelchair, but before they could put her into the Escalade, the nurse got some kind of emergency call, so you picked Cris up and placed her in the backseat yourself. When you had her cradled in your arms, Mrs. Lovejoy said, "Hey," and you looked up and smiled while she took your picture with her iPhone. And when you buckled Cris in her seat, she woke up. The Saint Christopher medal that Frank gave you was swinging free from your neck as you reached over her. Cris reached out and grabbed the medal, so you took it off your neck and put it around hers.

"What do you think would cause someone to do something like that?" you ask, keeping your eyes on the road ahead.

"Something like what? You mean exploding a bomb at the bottom of the ocean and cracking the world just about in half? Or preserving people's heads in jars?"

You don't answer because you don't know what you mean.

"Evil," Mrs. Lovejoy says. "There is such a thing as evil, you know. True evil. Pure evil. That's what the death penalty is for. To exterminate true evil. For every action there is an equal and opposite reaction."

"Newton's third law."

"Right. If you create evil, society's reaction is to exterminate it."

"What about chaos theory?" you say. Because you feel that evil has influenced your life since day one, but you did not invite it into your life. "What if you created evil unintentionally?"

"What do you mean?"

"If your actions cause reactions that you have no control over. If you try to do something good but end up with something bad."

"That's bullshit, we're all responsible for our own actions. Look, there's been an accident."

Up ahead you see Chandler's obese body sprawled along the roadside, next to the Cutlass, which is stopped at an odd angle. Frank is waving his arms, obviously in distress, trying to flag you down. Your foot depresses the brake pedal and the car slows.

"What are you doing? Don't slow down. Keep going. What are you doing? Don't stop."

"I have to. I think that man's hurt."

"No. I'll call on my phone. I'll call for help."

MRS. LOVEJOY

What is wrong with Billy? Why is he stopping? You told him not to stop. You never stop for strangers on a road. That fat man must have had a heart attack. You've never seen anybody so fat. You're in an Escalade. Might as well have a CARJACK ME bumper sticker. But this is the mountains. People in the mountains don't carjack each other. That's Atlanta. People here help each other. People here are different.

Billy stops the SUV, cuts the engine, and takes the keys with him when he gets out. You wish he had just left the engine running. That would have been safer.

He walks up to the man who waved you down. The man is wearing long sleeves even though it is far too warm to be dressed that way. They talk for a minute. The man points at the fat man lying on the ground and nonchalantly pushes his sleeves up (because it really is hot out there), and you clearly see that his arms are covered in tattoos. That alarms you. Tattoos are so commonplace today, but still it disturbs you. Heightens your sense of concern. Something seems off here.

Billy points back to the car and the tattooed man points back at his friend on the ground like his friend is not an injured human being but simply some prop on a stage. It just seems so weird. Like this is a little play put on just for you. And the actors are unconvincing. Then the man lashes out. He strikes Billy in the face. You see

129

blood pour from Billy's nose, shockingly red in the mountain sunshine. And then the fat man is up. Surprisingly limber, surprisingly quick for such a large man. Through the windshield you watch him coming at you. It's like you're watching a movie at one of those drive-in theaters. And finally you move. You move.

Your purse. You need your purse. You claw through it looking for your phone. Where is it? Where in the name of God is it? Every time you look up, the fat man has stuttered closer like a strobe light at a spook show. You look back down and there it is. There is the phone. It is in your hand. And you look up and the fat man has strobed right up to your window. He is there leering at you. And you forgot to lock the doors after Billy got out. And just as the fat man pulls at the outside handle, you reach and hit the lock button. You are in time. You hear the satisfying sound of all four door locks engaging. And then the sound of the fat man pawing at the handle that won't open the door.

Through the passenger window you look the fat man in the eyes and there is nothing there. There is determination. Frustration. Anger even. But behind those surface emotions is a vast emptiness that horrifies you. Then he drops from view, and you know exactly what he's doing. Looking for a rock to break the window. This is the mountains. There are rocks everywhere.

You drop the phone, because it's too late for the phone. You could call for help, but that would give the fat man time to break the window, and by the time the responders got here, all they would find is three dead bodies. You, Cris, and Billy. You've got to get away. Escape. You turn the purse upside down and the contents spill out over the seat. All of the silly useless crap you stuff your purse with. The tissues, the pills, the gum, the makeup, the wallet, the loose change, the lotions, perfumes, the keys. *The keys.* The extra set of car keys. Right there. Right there on top. You are saved. You have saved yourself.

Then the passenger window explodes. Thousands of tempered-glass granules shower you like violent New Year's Eve confetti. If you had time to think, you would realize the safety glass is harmless, but you are not thinking—you are moving. The fat man reaches through the window frame, unlocks the door, and opens it. He reaches for you, but you are already on the other side of the seat behind the steering wheel and you stab the key into the ignition and it slides right in—just like God wants you to get away. God wants you to win because the car starts right up and in the movies it never starts right up. In the movies the battery is always dead.

The fat man has climbed most of the way into the vehicle. He grabs your right arm and wrenches it. He says, "Going somewhere, Sweet Pea?" You can smell his breath. It smells the way a puppy smells. And with your awkward left hand you reach across yourself and drag the gear shift into drive and simultaneously push the gas pedal to the floor. You turn the wheel to the left and keep the gas floored and the force of acceleration pulls the fat man out of the car, through the open passenger door. Except he still holds on to your right arm so he is pulling you out with him. You straighten up the vehicle and the Escalade lurches into a field. You see Cris in the rearview and wonder how she can still be asleep and you thank God she is strapped into her booster seat because the field is rocky and jerks the SUV violently. Then the front wheels roll in and out of a drainage ditch and the vehicle reverberates so hard that it almost throws the man from the car. But he has your arm as an anchor. And you feel your shoulder dislocate. You hear it too. The pain is beyond anything you have ever felt, but you can not indulge it. Not now. The lower half of the fat man's body dangles out the open passenger door, and he has pulled you so far that you are no longer behind the wheel. You are no longer in control of the vehicle.

And it all comes to a sudden violent stop when the Escalade hits a sweetgum tree head on. The fat man loses his grasp on your now floppy arm, because it is not really attached to your body frame anymore, it is just kind of hanging there in a sack of flesh. He rolls out of the vehicle. Both air bags have deployed with an explosive stereophonic pop, and that is probably what saved you. The horn emits a continuous monotonous note. And in the backseat, Cris screams.

Like a zombie, the fat man crawls back up through the passenger door, over the deflated air bags, and you wonder what is propelling him, giving him this strength. You use your good left arm to pivot yourself around. You ratchet your leg back and strike the fat evil man full force in the face. He screams but holds on. And what is fueling him, you wonder. Hatred? That vast emptiness?

You turn your head because Cris's screaming is too much to ignore and then the evil fat man has your leg and he is pulling you, dragging you from the car. Your right arm is useless to you. But you are not quite ready to give up. No. You kick him again in the face. And he screams. His grip lessens enough for you to reach down to the floorboard and scoop up your phone. You scoot your body away from his mindless grasp. You open the driver's-side door and tumble out of the SUV. Your useless right arm (throbbing with the pain you refuse to indulge) ends up under you somehow and the weight of your falling body breaks the bone. You hear it snap. Sounds like a tree branch. No, it sounds like the snap of a really good chocolate bar. One with high cacao content. Quite crisp. There is no pain. All pain has vanished. You are lying in a field under a sweetgum tree, your arm broken, your shoulder dislocated, and you can feel spiky prickly sweetgum burr balls digging into your cheek. This is your reality.

And 911 is such an easy number to dial, but the horror-movie reality catches up with you now, because your stupid panicked fingers keep pressing the wrong numbers and you have to clear it and start over. And by then the evil fat man has crawled through the Escalade and is about to pour out of the driver's side door on top of you. You roll out of the way and stagger to your feet and you start to run. Not only can you feel your broken dislocated arm dangling and bouncing like a rubber toy as you run, but you feel a sweetgum burr stuck to your cheek like Velcro. You are about to wipe it off when you run right into the tattooed arms of the man who beat up Billy. He's wearing some kind of flesh-tone latex mask. He plucks the phone from your hand and tosses it over his shoulder. He looks you in the eyes and you are so grateful to not be met by a vast emptiness there. He holds you at arm's length. For a second you think he is going to kiss you. But instead, his rough fist hits you in the side of the head.

Losing consciousness is not the fast lights-out sensetion you always imagined it might be. Instead, it is very slow, like a dimmer switch on a chandelier. The last genuinely conscious thing you feel is the spiky hurtful sweetgum burr detach from your cheek. And the last genuinely conscious thing you hear is the braying car horn and you also hear Cris's hysterical screams. And you hear them for a very long time. Until that dimmer switch fades and mingles them into a single sibilant sound that is quite a bit like a telephone dial tone.

FRANK

You rub the ointment onto Billy's side. He fell on a sharp rock when you hit him. It looks bad. Deeply bruised and seeping blood and watery plasma at the center.

You are weaning yourself off the speed. It has to stop. Your mind. Stardust. Ha-ha. But you still have some in your front pocket in case things get bad.

Here you sit in a filthy trailer with no running water and a propane electricity generator. Here you sit as an adult in the home of the man who molested you as a child. Here you sit, taking care of Billy and you are asking yourself why you are drawn to him. Why have you burned and maimed and murdered others in the name of protecting Billy. You rub the salve into his side, your fingers greasy slick.

Why? Why have you abducted a child for ransom money? To take another child to Canada? What will you find there? What will you do to Billy there? Who are you? What is inside you?

Here you sit in the aftermath of what just might be the worst-planned kidnapping in the history of kidnapping. Like those criminals you see in the Weekly World News. Criminals so genetically stupid it's a wonder they can tie their own shoes. The punk who holds up a bar and it turns out it's a cop bar. The bank robber who catches a city bus for his getaway car. The

135

dealer who calls the cops to report that his stash has been stolen. That's what this is.

Your slick fingers probe the wound and Billy winces. You look up at him. His eye is purpleblack and swollen.

"Sorry. I know it hurts."

"Not too bad."

You lightly apply more ointment, more than is needed, and Billy winces again.

"Sorry."

You stare at the wound. The abraded skin. The dark pucker at the center. And you remember when you were the boy sitting in the chair. When your eye was purpleblack and swollen. When Chandler anointed you. When you had cuts and bruises and cigarette burns on your body. Your father's punishments. And Chandler's love. Maybe he was a predator, but you were hurt and scared and had no one else to turn to. You were grateful for Chandler, for his affection, his protection, his love. And if there was some way for you to show him that you loved him too, that you valued him, that you wanted to make him glad to have you around, well, you did it.

And you rub the ointment and Billy is moaning, hot tears spill down his face. You should stop but you don't. You are hurting him. You whisper:

"I'll take care of you."

And Billy cries even harder. Except he is you and you are him and you are Chandler and we are stardust.

"Don't you worry, Frank," you say. "My little Frankie."

And your hand drops lower, an oily slimy trail of blood and grease.

"Little Frankie. I'll take care of you."

And you are Frank, and you are Chandler, and you are Billy.

BILLY

For the first time ever you are glad to see Chandler.

Frank moves his hand away when he hears Chandler coming through the door, but not quite fast enough.

Chandler says, "Well, what a Norman Rockwell this would make. Oh my. My, my, my, my, my. Frank, I do believe you've got the fever for the flavor."

Frank tapes a rag to your side and you just don't know what is wrong with him. You wipe the tears from your face, careful of your black eye. Frank called you Frankie and his voice sounded like Chandler's and it was scary like a bad dream. And he hurt you. And touched you. You wonder who is Frank.

"I drove into Atlanta and put it in a public mailbox. I wore gloves. They should get it in two days. Maybe one."

Frank says, "Why don't we just buy one of those disposable cell phones?"

"Think, Frankie. It's not that hard. Those little phones have transmitters in them. It's not that hard of a concept. They *transmit*. Get it? They're phones. We'd have birds in the air all over this mountain. Just let me handle this. Stick with the plan, sugar britches."

The plan, from what you've been able to piece together listening to Frank and Chandler talk about it in that funny lip-smacking, throat-clicking, jaw-clenching way they talk is this: The note will ask for money for the safe return of "the boy and the girl." The idea is that the Lovejoys will think the kidnappers took you, too, because they mistakenly believe you are the Lovejoys' son—thus clearing you of suspicion. There are the usual threats about not contacting the police. The note tells them to put the money in a McDonald's bag (*that's all Steven Spielberg and shit*, Chandler has said about fifty times) and drop it in a public trashcan at Riverside Park Pavilion in downtown Helen at noon during the Indian Cultural Festival. The exact trashcan will have a red dot painted on it, and the McDonald's bag is supposed to have a red dot on it, too. Chandler will pay one of his kids to pay another kid to retrieve the bag. "It's a double buffer, Frankie. Double. Analog. Old school."

"That little girl is sick," Frank says. "If we had a phone, we could wrap this up and have her home by tomorrow."

"Frank, are you listening to me? No phones."

Like a gangster in an old black-and-white movie, Chandler parts the ratty curtains and peers sidewise through them. "Hell, I saw a transponder over the hill there."

"She still hasn't woke up. We need to hurry and get her back to her people."

You speak up, hoping you can bring some peace to this. "Mrs. Lovejoy said that the interferon treatments make Cris tired and sleepy, but she should be stronger when she wakes up."

"See, Frank? She's fine. It's all good in the hood. Stop being such a worry wart. Bump up and chill out."

"But she shouldn't be staying in Chandler's bed-room," you say.

"Look, Billy-Boy, you mind your place or Bessie'll mind it for you."

"Chandler won't hurt her, Billy. He loves kids. She's gonna be all right. You don't have to worry. We'll get the money, and before you know it we'll be fishing off the side of a glacier. Hunting elk and walking on snowshoes."

And then you cough. It comes out of nowhere. You don't feel a need to cough, you just cough. And blood splatters Frank's shirt. Like someone flicked a paint-brush, wet with red paint, at him.

"My stomach," you say.

Frank just looks at you. Then he reaches in his pocket and pulls out a little plastic bag. He blinks at the blood on his shirt and taps a tiny mound of dirtywhite powder onto the back of his fist and bumps up.

It's all good in the hood.

DETECTIVE JERNIGAN

Your sergeant gives you a lot of freedom. He knows your history and knows you won't embarrass the department, so he secured permission for you to poke around outside your jurisdiction. He understands that we're all on the same team. The drive out of Atlanta is a nice one. Peaceful. You and Burdick do not talk during the drive. You sip your coffee and relish not giving in to the burden of conversation.

She was asleep when you left the house this morning. She'll sleep until at least noon. You left a note saying that you had to leave the house early to drive to Stockmar County. You had told her as much the night before, but her memory is bad. You don't know if it's the depression that causes that, or the pills she takes to treat the depression.

It is only thirty minutes since dawn, but when you pull into the Stockmar County Sheriff's Office, it is busy with activity. Something is wrong.

Inside, you and Burdick wait at the front desk and listen while a deputy finishes up on the phone.

"Yes, ma'am. We appreciate the call. Anything at all. A terrible— I know you are, and we appreciate it." The deputy hangs up and his phone starts beeping just as soon as he does. He looks you and your partner up and down. "Thought the GBI was too busy to make it today.

What with that fella putting people's heads in jars and all you got goin' on."

"Excuse me?" you say.

"You two with the state bureau, ain't you?"

You pull out your shield. "I'm Detective Joseph Jernigan with the Atlanta Police Department, and this is—"

"Detective Mike Burdick," Burdick says and flashes his own badge because he likes to have his voice heard and not appear subordinate.

"We're here on a courtesy visit. Just wanted to alert you to our presence. There's a man—"

A door behind the front desk flies open and out of it bursts the sheriff.

"Hal! Why don't you answer the goddamn phone? When will you have the results from the vehicle? Guy's prints probably all over it."

Hal, the deputy you've been talking to looks back at the sheriff and says, "All the prints lifted from the Escalade are at the GBI lab. They said four p.m. today. Maybe later."

"Maybe later?"

"They're busy with that serial killer case. The jars. And these two men are detectives from Atlanta. Want to see you."

"Well, we just—" you start to explain.

"Atlanta? Why the fuck for?" The sheriff sighs and looks defeated. "Come in the office."

And you follow him.

Sheriff Anderson is tall, at least six-four, with a big belly and grey hair. He tells Burdick to close the door.

"Listen fellas, I appreciate it and everything, but you

should've called first. We're not Mayberry, for Christ's sake. I may not be Andy Taylor, but I'm sure as shit not Barney Fuckin' Fife. Like I say, I appreciate it, but we're okay. And why Atlanta cops? Who called you?"

"Is there maybe something going on here we don't know about?"

"How's that?"

"Sheriff, I don't know what you're talking about."

"You're not here 'cause of the abduction?"

"Abduction?"

"Jesus-in-a-side-car. I'm sorry."

The sheriff extends his hand and you shake it. Then he does the same for Burdick.

"I thought...It's been so crazy around here. The Lovejoys are—well listen, what can I help you with?"

Burdick speaks up. "There is a man living in Stockmar County, one John Chandler Norris, who we are investigating in connection with a vice operation in Atlanta."

You jump in. "And as a courtesy, we wanted to check in and let your deputies know we'd be asking questions and snooping around. We didn't really need to see you. Just a courtesy check-in."

"One a them perverts, huh? Yeah, we got us a few. Snoop all ya want. You can check with Belk out front, see what we got on file with him, but other than that, we kinda got our hands full. Any chance he could be involved in our abduction? A little girl, eight years old, and a boy—young man about eighteen."

"Highly unlikely. Norris's MO is a slow burn. Building relationships with children over time. Earning their trust. He's never advanced beyond child grooming and

145

enticement. Never snatched a child. And he typically targets boys. Prepubescent boys."

Burdick adds, "Although he will exploit young girls, pornographic images—"

"Child abuse images," you cut in. You prefer the current terminology. Also, it is more accurate.

"Child abuse images he can sell or trade," Burdick says, correcting himself and cutting his eyes at you. "But, no, he's never done anything violent. Never hurt a child physically."

"Still sounds like he ought to be locked up."

"He used to be. Now he's cured. Ha-ha," Burdick says.

"Thank you, Sheriff. Is there any way we can assist in your current situation?"

"No. It was a violent abduction. Beat the child's mother severely. No contact from the perpetrators, yet, but we expect a ransom demand. Wealthy family. GBI was called in for an assist, but they got their hands full with that nutcase in Valdosta puttin' peoples' heads in jars. People preserves. Goddamn ocean's cracked in half and boiling over with black tar oil and us human beings runnin' around like we can't kill each other fast enough and just what in God's name is this world comin' to?"

"Before we go," Burdick says, "the address we got for Norris on the sex offenders registry—can't get it to come up on our GPS. Like it doesn't exist."

"What is it?"

Burdick read from his notepad, "1300 Lynch Mountain Meadows."

Anderson nods and says, "Yep, that's just a clearing in a stand of woods at the base of Lynch Mountain.

Homeless camp there. People livin' in lean-tos and cardboard boxes. A little hobo camp. That's the address that goes into the computer for anyone who don't have anywhere to live. I'll draw you a map how to get there."

Yes, Norris is small time. The so-called "innocent" stuff. Barely a blip on the trafficking radar. Never explicit, yet intended to arouse. He sticks to the indica-tive/nudist category. The kind of thing every family photo album has at least a few of. But context is the key. Family snapshots are not sold on the Internet and masturbated over in locked rooms. Context. Sick, yes, repulsive, yes, but certainly nothing worth driving three hours for. Still, though, Norris is plugged into the network. They find each other. Even before the Internet, they always somehow managed to find each other. Network. Buy. Sell. Trade. They find each other. They know things. You want to talk to him. You want to know who he knows. See if he's got any fresh pictures. You hate the smell of Polaroid pictures. That plasticy odor and the sharp sting of the chemical reactants and the self-developing agents. That smell makes you angry. You just want to talk to Norris. See what he knows. Who he knows. He's a dough boy. He'll yield to your touch.

The shantytown looks just like you expect it to. Campfires and cardboard shacks. Plywood lean-tos. Plastic roofs and canvas sheeting. Every town's got a place like it, some big, and some small like this one. Even mountainfolk. But not many people ever see it. Shantytown. Niggertown. The Barrens. Dodge City. Hooverville.

You are obviously police, so nobody much wants to talk to you. You describe Norris (fat, white, gross) over and over. Finally you see recognition in one man's eyes. The man has lost several teeth, most likely from poor dental hygiene—you have to reposition yourself to stay upwind of his breath. He tells you that Norris was ostracized. Run out of the camp. These are people who have fallen victim to the hard times, the man tells you. The economy. Some folks are here with children. And Norris became too friendly. People didn't like it. Forced him out. He says there was talk of an empty trailer, in Chastain Holler right on the Chattahoochee River. Drug up there as a hunter's cabin, but abandoned, the man said, and maybe you all might want to take a look see.

And he drew you a map.

It's a good map. Through sweetgum and scrub pine, over rutted, crumbling asphalt that disintegrates into dirt roads, until you make your final left turn and there sits the trailer like a polyp on otherwise healthy skin. A Cutlass and some kind of old Datsun are parked beside the trailer—atypical moles that threaten to divide out of control. In the distance, storm clouds portend that this day will not end well.

BILLY

Cris is curled up next to you, and you are lying on the couch looking at your Canadian travel brochures. There are pictures of jagged rocky mountains, dusted in snow like something sweet from a bakery. Then photos of vast prairies that give way to ancient, continent-wide expanses of spruce, balsam fir, jack pine, white birch, and aspen. It says *the northern stretches of this region are home to Canada's boreal forest—one of the earth's last remaining relatively undisturbed forests large enough to maintain its biodiversity.* And that is where you will live. You know the air up there has got to be pure. And you wonder if Cris would thrive up there, too. Away from all the junk that makes her sick. You could fish from the clean rivers and you wouldn't have to worry about mercury contamination or PCBs that build up in the fish.

"This is where we're going to live," you tell Cris, and point at the picture of the boreal forest, even though you know she isn't looking or listening. She is sluggish. Groggy. Tired and out of it. But she will be okay. "Just me and Frank. He takes care of me. And I take care of him, too. Not in obvious ways, but in ways that are important. He needs me."

You want to burn something. You need a release. But there is nowhere to do it. You are good at hiding the smell, but you don't want to risk any smoke at all in the trailer in case it messes up Cris's breathing. You could go out in the woods, but you don't want to leave Cris by herself. But the brochures are working. They calm you, and they seem to soothe Cris too.

In the back of a kitchen drawer you found an old piece of candy. Butterscotch wrapped in yellow-orange cellophane. You're sure it's stale but probably still okay. You cleaned it up by rubbing it on your shirt and it is transformed into a shiny disc like the sun. Now you pull it out of your pocket and put it in Cris's hand. Or you try to. Her hand is clenched into a hard little fist and you can't pry it open to put the candy inside. Even if she doesn't want to eat it, you figure she might enjoy having something to hold on to. That it might bring her comfort.

"And after we build the cabin, we can lay out on a rock in the warm sun next to the river. But not too long, because there's a chunk missing out of the sky now, called the ozone hole, and it lets in the bad—"

There is a knock at the door and you put the brochures in your rear pants pocket. You put the butterscotch disc in your front pocket. You are about to run out the back door, but you don't want to leave Cris, because you don't know who is out there, and maybe they are going to try and break in. You are stuck. Frozen. Then a voice calls through the door, "Police." And what you do is take the blanket and cover Cris with it so that she is hidden. You open the door.

The man at the door shows you a gold badge in a little black wallet. He says, "Hello, I'm Detective Jernigan and this is Detective Burdick. May we come in?"

You have seen enough TV to know that you never ever tell the police it is okay to come into your home. It's like inviting a vampire inside. It gives them power.

"I'm not allowed to have people inside," you say, which seems pretty reasonable and not likely to instill suspicion.

"Could we speak with Chandler Norris please?"

"He's not here."

"Are you sure?"

You nod.

"When will he be back?"

"Should be in a couple of hours."

"Couldn't we just come inside and wait for him?"

You think of Cris hidden under the cover on the couch and you feel the muscles in your arm tighten in preparation for opening the door wide and letting the detectives inside, because what you are doing, what you are a part of, is wrong, but then you think about Frank and vast prairies and jagged mountains dusted like powdered sugar and the undisturbed biodiversity of the boreal forest. And you can see Frank emerging from the clean river, reclining on an oven-warm sun-baked slab of smooth river rock. He does not wear his artificial leg. He is naked and unashamed and made warm in the diffuse glow. And you join him there, naked and unashamed in the warm light.

"No," you say. "I'm not allowed."

"Son, how old are you?"

"Eighteen."

"Uh-huh. Well, you might want to be careful whose company you keep."

"Yes, sir," you say and close the door.

* * *

Frank and Chandler are sitting in lawn chairs in the
backyard. Particolored vinyl straps stretched across rust-
pitted aluminum frames. It is a wonder Chandler's chair
can hold him.

As you walk up, Frank says to Chandler, "Damn,
look at those clouds."

"Quite ominous looking, my boy, quite ominous."

You are always careful in how you approach the two
of them. They have taken to lounging around, long
hours of inactivity, but you've found that small disturbances can pierce that calm shell the way a pin pops a
balloon.

You clear your throat to announce your presence.
Chandler cranes his head on wattled neck flesh.

"Sweet William!"

"The police were here. They asked for Chandler."

Chandler stands and the lawn chair is stuck to his
backside. The aluminum frame is bowed and molded to
his flesh. He picks it off the way someone might pick
underwear out of their butt.

He turns to Frank and says, "Get the rope."

DETECTIVE JERNIGAN

The name of the roadside diner is actually The Greasy Spoon. You like that.

The waitress's name is Starla, and after you've both given Starla your orders, you tell Burdick to save your seat while you walk out to the parking lot. You prefer privacy when you make personal phone calls.

"Hey, it's me. You up?"

You listen to what she has to say. You hate the lethargy and apathy that is always in her voice. It's been so long now, you can't even remember what it was her voice used to sound like. And then you realize that you can't remember what your own voice used to sound like, either. Carefree? No, you're sure that you never sounded carefree. What an absurd word.

"I know," you say. "Me too. Are you sure you're okay? If it gets too bad you've got some of those other pills left. In the cabinet."

The wind is picking up, the temperature dropping. The blowing makes it hard to hear her on the other end.

"I'll be home tonight. Why don't you see if there's a good movie on TV? Maybe Lifetime. Okay. Me too. I better get off. Bad storm coming. I love you."

You press End and stand there at the edge of the parking lot, looking down into a trash-filled gorge. The shifting atmospheric pressure plays havoc inside your head.

* * *

At the booth in The Greasy Spoon, you find Burdick hunched over his phone. He's running some kind of map application and as he slides his finger over the screen, little text balloons pop up.

"Just checking the area on the registry map," he says. "Got one Uday Rajaguru. Possession of child pornography. Currently employed as a gardener."

"Birds of a feather."

"Might as well check. Stir them up a little bit."

Starla sets your plates down and says, "Y'all enjoy that."

FRANK

You stand outside the trailer. The wind is blowing leaves and pine needles from the trees. You look over and see Billy holding the girl wrapped in a blanket, cradled in his arms. She is somewhere between sleep and coma. A clenched fist dangling from the cloth folds is the only real sign of life.

Chandler walks up to you, his black caftan or muumuu or housedress or whatever it is, flowing around him like Lawrence of fucking Arabia. He's carrying a shovel in one hand, and with his other hand he drags a thirty-two-gallon Rubbermaid tote. From inside the tote Chandler pulls out a five-foot section of garden hose. He uses a box cutter to carve an X in the lid of the tote, and he feeds the section of hose through it. A breathing tube. This is Plan B.

"Where's the rope?"

You open the Cutlass's trunk using the key. The nylon cord is in there, coiled and ready. There is Chandler's Colt .45, nestled in the center of the coil. Bessie. Like the head of a sleeping snake. And you remember. You remember. The convenience store. Shop N Save. You were still a kid. Chandler wouldn't carry a gun. He was afraid of guns then. Squeamish. And that makes you realize that Chandler really is different since they gave him the shock treatment, but he was never a good guy.

* * *

You stand together at the counter. Chandler sets a forty-ounce Miller Lite next to the register and asks the man behind the counter for a carton of More 120s. When the man turns to reach for the cigarettes, Chandler hands you the forty. You take aim, then shatter the heavy bottle at the base of the man's skull. He goes down. Even then, you were prone to violence. You were different from other people. Something inside you was missing. You would cut, and kick, and shoot, and break and stomp and hurt and twist and tear, and you never thought twice about it. That was the way God had made you. Or maybe it was the way your father made you. It didn't matter. You didn't feel it.

Chandler helps you over the counter. On the other side, your foot slides in the pool of beer and blood that has oozed across the floor and you go down. You get back up and punch the No Sale key on the register. You grab all the cash and hand it to Chandler and it disappears into the folds of the material that drapes his body.

You pull the gun and the rope from the trunk. You shove the gun through your pants waist and hand the rope to Chandler.

"Frankie, I want you to stay here. Don't open the door. Just keep watch. We need to know if we have visitors." Chandler, the folds of his garment whipping around him, turns to Billy and says, "Okay, let's go."

You pull the Colt from your waist and level it at

Chandler's head, stopping him cold. Your mind is as conflicted and uncentered as the weather.

"Don't let me down. Not again."

"Moi? Bitch, please. You're not making sense." But he knows. He understands.

Chandler reaches across the counter and gives you a hand, pulling you out of there. But the cashier is up on his knees and he grabs your shirt tail. He pulls you back and you fall on top of him, both of you covered in a rusty mixture of beer and blood.

Chandler has waddled to the door, looking back at you. "C'mon, Frank!" he says—an impatient parent scolding a lackadaisical child. You hit the clerk in the head with your fist and scramble back over the counter. You are free, on the other side, except the son of a bitch has latched onto your shirt tail again, and you can't get traction, your feet spinning like a cartoon road runner in the beerblood that has spread from behind the counter all over the floor.

Chandler is waving you forward like you are dawdling over the selection of chewing gum instead of caught by the clerk. The man has you with one hand, and when you look back over your shoulder you see that the clerk, blood streaming down his neck, is reaching under the counter with his other hand. And he comes up with a sawed-off shotgun. The man doesn't even hesitate, he just takes aim at your leg, the knee area, and gives you both barrels. It's like a stick of dynamite went off. A six-inch section in the middle of your leg just vaporizes. The man lets go of your shirt and you fall to the floor in a deaf bloody heap.

While you are waiting for the pain to hit you, you look down to your right and see that the bottom half of your leg is separated from your body. It's still wearing a scuffed black leather boot at one end, and at the other you can see the shredded denim of your blue jeans and white bone and ragged scorched flesh.

Beyond your leg you can see the clerk struggling to reload the shotgun, but he is shaking too hard, too jittery to do it. You look in the other direction, still deaf, still no pain, and there is Chandler. You cry out for him to help you, but you can not hear your own voice and neither apparently can Chandler because he turns his back on you and pushes his way out the door.

And then the pain hits you. It is spiritual.

"I am making sense. You know exactly what I mean."

"Mean, Frankie?" Chandler brushes the gun away from his face as though it were a mosquito.

"You left me in that store. Bleeding out on the floor. My leg blown off."

Leaves and debris and occasional fat cold drops of rain are darting around the two of you.

"Frankie, I had no choice."

"My leg. My fucking leg."

"My hands were tied."

"You lie."

"Be reasonable. Now is not the time."

"No, now is the time. Now."

"You break my heart, Frank. I've always loved you

like a son. I took you in. You were just a boy. I raised you like a father would. When your real father wouldn't. Who do you come to when you're in trouble? Me. It's always been me. You've always been with me, Frankie."

"You took me in. You fixed my father. I owe you. I'll always owe you. But you left me in that store. I won't leave Billy. I won't make the same mistake you made."

"The sins of the father, is that it?"

You put the gun back through your belt.

"I'm going, too. All three of us." And you realize that you love Chandler. You could never hurt him.

Chandler leads, carrying the empty green Rubbermaid tote. Billy carries the girl. And you are last, using the shovel like a cane, picking your way across the creek and following on into the woods.

DETECTIVE JERNIGAN

This time Burdick's GPS takes you exactly where you want to go. A ritzy house with nice gardens, and it looks like the grounds are maintained like a golf course.

You talk to a Mexican kid who is hurrying to put down fertilizer before the rain starts. His English is non-existent, but when you say Rajaguru, recognition lights his dark eyes and he points to a four-bay garage up near the house.

You knock on a side entrance of the structure and a small Indian man opens the door. You flash the shield and fear springs up in the little man's face. And then recognition. Briefly, escape. And finally, resignation.

BILLY

Chandler's humming really bothers you. Nursery rhymes. It's like he's in a good mood. Like his spirits are uplifted. The three of you are going to bury a small child in the woods. Bury her alive. It is not a time for humming or high spirits.

He hands Frank a piece of white chalk.

"Here. We don't want to make the same mistake as Hansel and Gretel. You'll find out what lost is. Mark a tree every time I tell you.

You are tired and you sit down for a minute, Cris resting in your lap. Frank is far stronger than you. He should be the one to carry Cris, but you want it to be you. And it is harder for him to get around in the woods with his leg.

Frank marks the peeling paper bark of a Birch tree with a white chalk slash.

"Let's go, Mr. Man," Chandler says to you.

You get to your feet and march deeper into the woods. The wind is calmer now, and you can hear rain in the canopy of tree crowns above, but it is not yet falling to the loamy earth.

A flash of lightning illuminates what you are doing, and thunder follows in protest.

DETECTIVE JERNIGAN

You are breathing through a handkerchief because of the odor. It's not strong; in fact it's very faint. Probably been several days since a batch was cooked here. But you know from your stint on the Narcotics Enforcement Unit that the chemicals can linger for weeks and turn your lungs into Swiss cheese. You're careful about touching any surfaces for the same reason. That shit can migrate right through your skin. It sticks to walls, furniture, clothing. Once inside you, it targets your organs.

Uday Rajaguru sits at a small desk where he presumably keeps track of worker hours, places orders for equipment and supplies, and whatever else might be required of a man of his position. Like the Mexican boy you talked to outside, Uday is probably an illegal. He offered no protest when you pushed your way into the garage. He's made no commotion or whined about his "rights."

At first, you passed the ether smell off as starter fluid. Just one of the odors you could expect in a garage workshop with mowers and small engine machines. Maybe the tell-tale rotten egg odor was from a lingering beer fart. It happens. But you add in the sharp ammonia twang, and there's just no way around it. Someone's been cooking meth.

"Uday, listen, you want to mix up the occasional batch of bathtub speed, hey, far as I'm concerned, have at it. Knock yourself out. That's not my concern. That is not why I'm here today. Not my circus, not my monkeys." All of which is true, but you have every intention of stopping back by the sheriff's office on your way out of town to alert them to the possible existence of a methamphetamine lab. Chemicals from byproduct fumes could be leaching into the main house, poisoning the family that lives there. Wreaking havoc with their health.

"No, Uday, we're here today to talk about photography."

"I am rehabilitated," he says in a thick accent. *Rah-hee-beel-ee-tated.*

"We know you're rehabilitated, Uday. We know that. And we're not here to dig up the past. Not at all."

Burdick jumps in with, "And your wife. I bet she knows you're rehabilitated too." Which is not helpful. It breaks your rhythm and puts Uday on more of a defensive track than you wanted him. At this point, you want Uday to see light—a way out—not more darkness.

"Why do you persecute me? I have done nothing wrong. I am a good worker." *Peerseecute.*

"And that's what we'll tell your employer. And your parole officer. That you're a good worker. That you're rehabilitated. That you're not cooking crystal."

"Why do you do this to me? I don't hurt nobody."

"Do you know John Chandler Norris?"

"Maybe I think I need lawyer?"

"And where the fuck are you going to get a lawyer, Uday?"

"Know what they do to your kind in prison?"

ABNORMAL MAN

"Or India. Indian prison, if you should get deported. You and your wife."

Uday does something with his eyes, which you take to be an internal struggle. A moral reckoning. But it's difficult to know how much of it is play-acting. Calculated.

"I am so ashamed," he says and buries his face in his hands. "So ashamed. I have the picture. He make me take."

Uday has rolled the dice. He's kinda-sorta admitting that he has lewd and or pornographic images of children. This makes sense, though. It's simple possession. He does not create this type of material on his own. Never has. He just buys it. And he realizes that even if the cops play dirty and don't let him walk in exchange for information, he is in a far better position copping to the possession of indecent images than running a meth lab.

"Have you ever bought pictures from Norris?"

Morally, you made the decision long ago that the tradeoff was worth it. Letting the little monsters go so you could catch the big monsters. The world, you knew, was disappointingly full of men like Uday. Men who had secret stashes on their computers, in safety deposit boxes, under their mattresses—stashes that they took out in dim rooms and masturbated to. Sometimes, you knew, these stashes were handed down from father to son. They are sick pathetic weak human beings, each of whom you would be happy to crush under the heel of your shoe, leaving behind only a faint red smear that would disappear with time. But you can't do that. And these men are far too common to erase. They are just

167

weaklings who hide in the dark with their perversion that they would rather indulge than let go. They are not the big monsters. They do not entice children. They do not molest children. They do not photograph and video-tape and film children. They do not steal childhoods. Except, of course, they do.

If Uday gives up Chandler, will you really let him walk? You'll decide that later.

You repeat the question. "Have you ever bought pictures from Norris?"

Uday looks uncertain. Trying to make up his mind.

"It's okay," Burdick says. "We're not after you. We want Norris. You won't get into any trouble."

Which for once you are glad Burdick spoke up. It's on him. On his soul. Caught in the devil's bargain. Welcome to it, Burdick.

Uday reaches under the knee hole of his small work desk. He retrieves a manila envelope that had been taped to the underside of the drawer and hands it to Burdick.

"From Chandler." *Shandleer.*

Burdick shuffles through the Polaroids—my God but pedophiles love Polaroid cameras—and then hands them to you. You look through them. It is not the hard stuff. You are glad for that. It is a series of photographs of a young girl in provocative, playful poses. If these were in a family picture album, no one would think twice about any of them. The single most revealing shot shows the girl in a pair of panties without a top. She appears to be asleep in all of them. This is low-grade stuff. And in its way, you find it far more disturbing than the hardcore material. Because as disturbing as the explicit images are, at least you can connect the dots in some crude fashion.

At least you can somewhat understand that videos and photos of children posed or engaged in sexual situations still has a sexual element to it. There is provocation. But with these childhood poses, you just cannot on any level comprehend that an image of a sleeping child propped up by a stuffed animal could evoke a sexual response in an adult human being.

You imagine what Uday would look like under the heel of your shoe. The sound his bones would make as you crushed them. The red smear he would leave behind.

You slide the Polaroids back inside the envelope. You reflect on the disturbing aspect that the girl is asleep in all of them. Propped up. Posed. But asleep. Pale skin. With dark circles under her eyes. Like she might have been drugged. Or recently been sick.

You do not yet know it, but the girl in the photographs is Crisium Lovejoy.

BILLY

The rain comes down so hard you can hardly breathe. The ground is sodden and it sucks at your shoes, making it hard to walk. There doesn't seem to be any purpose to the path that Chandler chooses. He turns, goes forward, goes backward, and snaps his fingers at Frank whenever he wants a tree marked with chalk.

He stops and drops the plastic tote. He motions to Frank for the shovel. Chandler takes the shovel, then holds it out to you. You shake your head.

You realize that Chandler must wear makeup because mascara has melted around his eyes and is running down his face.

"I'm holding Cris."

"You little fuck. Take the shovel."

"No."

"You better have a talk with your little buddy, Frankie. He's playing with fire."

Frank doesn't say anything. He is picking at the pimple on his face. The pimple he has picked at so much that now it looks infected.

Chandler thrusts the shovel, almost hitting you. "I said take it."

You shake your head and a hundred yards away lightning strikes a tall pine tree, splitting it in half, right down the middle, and the three of you watch the tree fall and smell the smoke and ozone as it wafts down to you.

"See," Chandler says. "God don't like ugly." And he starts to dig. "When we get back, I'm going to show you what pain is, my little friend."

"I'm already in pain."

"No. But you will experience it. You will know it." He stares you down and the black drip of mascara running down his face disturbs you.

You start coughing, issuing a red mist from your mouth.

You turn to Frank.

"Frank, we can't do this. It's wrong."

"She won't get hurt. It's only for a little while. In case the police come to look for her."

"She's sick."

Frank takes out his little baggie of powder, bends over to shelter it from the rain, and bumps up from the end of his car key.

He sniffs and says, "It's only for a little while. We can't really back out now. We've done it. We can't take her back and call the whole thing off. Just for a little while, okay? This will get you what you want."

"I want it to stop."

You hear the sharp snick of the shovel blade cutting into the wet earth.

DETECTIVE JERNIGAN

You maneuver the sedan through the rain and pass the turnoff to return to Chandler Norris's trailer.

"Missed the turn," Burdick says.

"We gotta stop by the SO"

"Why?"

"What do you mean, 'why?'"

"I mean why are we going back to the Sheriff's Office?"

"So we can tell him that we're going to arrest Norris," you say. "And they can send someone out to arrest the Iranian."

"I believe Mr. Rajaguru is Indian. And I thought we promised him a pass if he gave up Norris."

"I changed my mind. He's a pervert. And he's running a meth lab."

"Doubtful. Maybe he cooks a little, but I'd hardly call it a lab. It just smelled like a groundskeeper's shed to me. Fertilizer and fumes."

Burdick shrugs. That shrug says a lot of things to you. Things you don't care to hear. Fuck him. Fuck Burdick.

"I know you know about me," you say. It's something you should have said a long time ago.

There is only the sound of the wipers, wheels on wet pavement, and rain battering the car.

"Yeah. I know. I'm sorry."

"Don't be sorry. Just back me up."

"I always back you up," Burdick says. "And you need to let me talk sometimes."

"I'm sorry."

"Don't be. Just back me up."

BILLY

"...N-G-O...B-I...N...G-O...and Bingo was..."

The hole is deep. Filling with muddy water. The shovel strikes into it one final time and lifts out mud and root debris.

"His name-o."

Out of breath, wet and mudstreaked, Chandler tosses the shovel aside. He picks up the empty Rubbermaid tote and wedges it into the hole. It doesn't quite fit, but you can see he is tired and not willing to widen the hole anymore. He pushes down and jiggles it, forces it using his bodyweight, until finally it slips out of sight beneath the ground.

Chandler turns to you, his arms outstretched. You sit against the trunk of a tree, Cris in your lap. You look at Chandler and shake your head.

"No," you say.

"What do you mean, 'no?'"

"I mean no."

You appraise Chandler's face. There is a vacancy there. He has excused himself from the reality of what he is doing. And you understand that at this point he could do anything. Kill you. Kill Cris. You doubt Frank could stop him. You doubt Frank would try to stop him. For it seems that Frank, too, has excused himself from this present reality. Frank has jumped down a rabbit hole of white powder to escape.

"I mean that I'll do it. Let me do it."

"Well, could you hurry the fuck up and do it?"

You carry Cris to the hole. You are going to nestle her into the Rubbermaid container, but you see that water has got into the bottom of it. Dark dirty water. You lay her on the ground and start scooping the water out with your hands.

"There's no time for that."

"She'll drown."

"Christ on the cross! She has the hose for air. She'll just get a little wet."

"Fuck you," you say. "You don't know what wet is."

And you resume drying out the inside of the container. Chandler must have heard something in your voice, because he walks away from you. And after a minute you've got most of the water out, but it seems like it just creeps back in, and you hear Chandler say your name, a repentant whisper.

"Billy-Boy?"

You look up and the shovel blade catches you full in the face, just under your jaw. And you are out.

When you wake up, it feels like only a little bit of time has passed. Frank is patting your cheek. Rousing you. And you wonder what happened to your protector. Why isn't he disemboweling Chandler with the shovel? But you know why. It is because he loves Chandler. In you, Frank sees himself as he might have once been, even if for just a moment. And he wants to protect that. But in Chandler he sees the man who is his fatherprotector-lover. And you can never be more important than that.

Chandler picks Cris up from the ground. "My sweet," he says and gives her an air kiss the same way a housewife might pretend-kiss a roast before popping it in the oven.

You crawl over to the hole and look down at Cris curled in the container. The right side of your face is swollen and it's hard for you to swallow. You remember the butterscotch in your pocket. You reach down and pry open her furled fingers and place the sun-colored candy inside her clenched fist.

Chandler snaps the lid on and feeds the section of garden hose through the X cut on the top. He drops the shovel inches from your face where you lay on the ground.

"Guess who's going to shovel now?"

You pick up the shovel and struggle to your feet.

"And if you even think about taking a swing at me with that thing, I'll kill you and put you in the box with the girl."

And how could it have come to this? What sequence of events has led you to these dim wet woods and put a shovel in your hand with which to bury alive a small child? A butterfly flaps its wings in China and a hurricane forms off the coast of Florida. Is it chaos? Or is it fate? What brought you here? Were the choices yours, or did something outside of you conspire to bring you here? Did a butterfly flap its wings, and that puff of air is what carried you here?

Unforeseen and unpredictable.

In other words, not your fault.

"Okay, Billy. My boy. Shovel."

And you do. Wet shovelful after wet shovelful you

dump onto the box, filling the hole. Your head is throbbing, and something inside you feels broken. The swelling in your face has affected your throat, constricted it. You have to swallow over and over to keep it open or your throat will swell shut.

The hole fills up quicker than it emptied. Of course. And when you are finished you step away from it. The wound in your side feels torn open again. You cough up blood, the cough forces your swollen throat open, and you keep swallowing so it stays open, your face on fire with pain. You turn around to look at Crisium Lovejoy's grave. And it is all too much. You pass out again.

You wake up after what is probably only a minute or two. You still have to swallow to keep your throat open.

Hunched over the filled-in grave, Chandler cries. He rubs at his face and what little of the mascara that is left smears like ash and charcoal. He is sitting there next to the garden-hose air tube jutting up out of the earth, crying, and Frank goes to him and puts his hand on his shoulder.

"I didn't used to be like this, Frank. You know that. I never hurt anybody. Not my children. My mind is like that tree over there. It's split in half. From a lightning bolt sent down out of the sky by God. Frank, what did they do to my mind in that Frankenstein castle? I didn't used to be this way. I was bad, but I was good inside. Inside my head, I was good."

"I know."

You look at Chandler and imagine what it would be like to crush him like a bug under the heel of your shoe. You close your eyes and swallow.

DETECTIVE JERNIGAN

You pull the sedan into the parking lot and see Sheriff Anderson coming out the front door. You park and run through the rain to catch him before he gets in his car. He sees you, gestures, and you both get inside his vehicle out of the rain.

"Lucky you caught me. Going home for dinner, bath, and bed. In that order."

"Anything on your abduction?"

"Just that it's fucked. GBI'll be here in the morning. No note. Wish there was a note. That'd make me feel better."

"Any chance the child's father is involved? Divorce looming? Custody issues?"

"Doubtful. He's in China."

"Well, we just wanted to let you know that we're going to pick up Chandler Norris. Manufacture and distribution of child abuse images."

You hand Anderson the packet of Polaroids.

"From Uday Rajaguru. He's in your registry. Caretaker at some kind of golf course. Smells like maybe he's been cooking meth up there."

You notice that Anderson's face drains of color as he flips through the photos, but most people react that way.

"We want to take Norris with us, but your men can pick up Rajaguru. If nothing else, be aware and—"

"It's her," Anderson says. "This is her."

BILLY

You keep getting up and pulling back the curtains to look out the window. Frank and Chandler think you're checking for police, but you're not. You're looking for the moon. The storm is winding down and the clouds are breaking up, so the moon should be out there. The moon would calm you. Because out in the woods, in a box buried in the ground, there is a little girl who has no hope of seeing the moon tonight. The moon has forsaken her as well.

You sit on the couch with Chandler. He just finished watching *New Zoo Review*, and now he's watching *The Wiggles*. Your face throbs, throat hurts. Frank sits at the kitchen table racking up lines. You lost your Bic and are trying to figure out a way to sneak either Frank's or Chandler's lighter, so you can start a fire in the bathroom. Chandler lights one of his More 120s, but he puts the lighter and cigarette pack back in the folds of his muumuu.

Outside, a dog barks. Just a single yelp. You look at Frank and Frank looks at Chandler. There should not be a dog out there. Everything is quiet, frozen in time. You hear a tiny creaking sound at the front door. Maybe it is the sound of the aluminum contracting. And then the glass in the front window shatters like someone threw a brick through it. But what lands on the floor is not a brick. It is an oblong black metal canister. The three of you stare at it. And you can actually read what it is, because in little white stenciled letters across the top it says STUN GRENADE. And then the world goes white. You are blind. And you are deaf. The world has evaporated. You exist in a vacuum, wrapped in cotton, hermetically sealed. And then there are hands on you. Shoving you. Hitting you. You are facedown on the floor, a heavy knee on your back, pinning you there like a bug. You feel plastic cable ties slipped around your wrists and pulled brutally tight.

You are caught.

BILLY

Through the broken-out window, you can see Frank and Chandler lined up outside the trailer, standing in the rain, their hands bound behind their backs with police zip ties. Frank looks scared. He looks guilty. But Chandler looks serene, at peace. Two sheriff's deputies stand guard.

You are sitting on the couch. Your hands, too, are bound behind your back. The police immediately identified you as the weakest link and separated you from Frank and Chandler. Sheriff Anderson and two detectives are talking to you, trying to reason with you. They keep mentioning "the right thing to do" and how this can all still turn out okay and you don't want this on your record or on your soul.

One of the deputies, his name is Belk, uses some kind of metal rod to pop the deadbolt on Chandler's bedroom door and then disappears inside.

A detective, you think his name is Jernigan, talks about how you are just as much a victim here as Crisium Lovejoy and how if you save her, you can save yourself.

And then Deputy Belk is standing there and he says, "Sheriff, I think you should look at this."

Sheriff Anderson pulls you along with him, and you enter Chandler's bedroom. You have never been in here before. And like Deputy Belk and Sheriff Anderson, and the two detectives who peer in from the door frame—

you are silent. Nobody quite knows what to say.

Balloon-print curtains in bright primary colors. A Power Rangers bedspread with matching sheets and pillowcase. Legos. Hot Wheels. An Easy Bake Oven. Polaroids of smiling children tacked to a bulletin board. A blackboard with the word CAT written in chalk. Finger paintings, one of which reads: I LOVE YOU CHANDLER.

It's a child's room. With no child.

"Oh my dear God," the sheriff says and walks over to the bulletin board and stops himself from pulling down a Polaroid of Crisium Lovejoy. "He has her. He sure as shit has her. Make no mistake."

The detective, Jernigan, steps in and gently grabs your arm at the elbow. "Let me talk to the boy," he says to Sheriff Anderson, and pulls you backward, out of the room.

"You better talk to him, Detective." The sheriff says. "You just better. Cause I'm done with it. I served in motherfuckin' Iraq."

The detective pulls you into the living room, and through the open front door you can see Mrs. Lovejoy push her way through the deputies stationed out front. She is loud and violent and the deputies don't have the heart to physically restrain her. And then she is inside and you are face to face with her. And you can tell that she is about to embrace you because she thinks you have been saved and if you have been saved then maybe Cris has been saved. But then she sees how the detective has you by the arm, pulling you. And she sees the curlicue strips of plastic that curl from your plasticuffs. And then she understands. You have not been saved. No, you have not been saved. You are what the world needs saving from. She slaps you. You are glad of it. You are glad for the throbbing pain her blow has reawakened in your jaw and throat. And then she is past you heading for the sheriff. The detective pulls you out the door and down the steps and from inside the trailer you hear Mrs. Lovejoy scream. And you realize that she has seen Chandler's bedroom.

The detective pulls you past Frank and Chandler standing in the rain. Past a patrol car through the window of which you can see your old boss, Uday, handcuffed in the backseat.

"I'm watching you, Billy-Boy." Chandler sings out, mocking. Then, loud enough to penetrate the patrol unit, "You too, Uday, you lying bastard!"

Inside, the detective's sedan is warm and dry. He uses a blade to cut off the plasticuffs. A police radio crackles, and there is a black shotgun locked muzzle-up into a rack between the seats. The dancing green LEDs from the scanner light up Detective Jernigan's face in a way that comforts you. It reminds you of the green radium glow of the instrument panel in your father's—your real father's—Chevelle SS, and how that green glow bathed his face on the ride home from Gatlinburg when you were still little. How your mother's hand rested in his lap. That was before everything changed. Coming home from the Great Smoky Mountains was the night you first realized that the moon followed you. You remember watching it through the tinted rear window. You look out the window now, hoping to draw comfort from it, but there is no moon tonight.

"Listen to me, son. Listen close. This can all still turn out all right. Just give me the story straight. Just tell me the truth. Do you know where the girl is?"

You shake your head. You can see Frank out there standing in the rain, and you are torn between what you want and what is right.

"I want you to look at this."

The detective pulls out an envelope. A little packet. He opens it and extracts what you already know is a photograph. You can tell just by looking at the back of it that it's a Polaroid picture. *Wetpopwhirr.*

The detective holds it out to you, face down. You make no move to reach for it.

"Take it," he says. "You have to take it."

And that's true. You do have to take it. So you do, and it is in your hand. Oilywetslick alive.

"Look at it."

It burns your eyes *Wetpopwhirr* because of course *Wetpopwhirr* it is a *Wetpopwhirr* picture of Cris.

You hand it back to the detective, but he won't take it from you. It's like he's making you hold it as punishment. You drop it on the seat.

"You know it's not mine."

"We know that, son. We found these in the possession of the Lovejoy's gardener, Uday Rajaguru." He scatters all of the Polaroids across the seat. He wants to hurt you with them. The corner of one rests against your thigh, and you draw yourself in so that it doesn't touch you. "He says he purchased them in trade from Chandler Norris. Norris says it's the other way around. You have to tell us what you know."

You look outside and still there is no moon. The

moon has deserted you. You have offended it. Shamed it.

You take a deep breath and say, "In any sufficiently complex environment, any action, even a simple one, will create a series of chain reactions that are unforeseen and unpredictable."

"What was that?"

"I'm not responsible. It's chaos. One single action can set off a series of events we have no control over."

"You have control. We're all responsible for our own actions."

You look at the pictures spread out in front of you and you say, "No. We have no control. It's chaos."

"I want to show you something," he says and takes out his wallet. He pulls a photograph from it. Not a Polaroid. A photograph. A portrait. A school picture. Wallet size. This photo he does not offer up for you to hold. This one he shows to you but keeps to himself.

"She was nine in this picture. Nine forever. For me. Alive. Dead. I don't know. Maybe she was molested. I don't know."

He puts the picture back in his wallet. Away from you.

"This is the most pain I'll ever have."

Outside there is Chandler and there is Frank and there is no moon.

"Don't be a part of this much pain. You have control."

BILLY

The beams of their flashlights are like lasers cutting through the ground-fog that rises from the saturated forest floor. You lead the sheriff and a line of his deputies deeper into the woods. To Cris.

What you have not yet told them, what you are afraid to tell them, is that you are lost. Hopelessly, utterly lost. Chandler was right about Hansel and Gretel. Just as the birds went behind Hansel and Gretel and ate their trail of breadcrumbs, the rain has come behind you and washed away the chalk marks.

You tell Anderson this, but all he says is, "You better look harder, boy." And when he senses that you truly are lost, that you are backtracking and wandering, he takes you aside and says, "If you don't find her, you will not come out of these woods alive. I personally will put a bullet in the back of your brain as you try to escape. I am an expert rifleman. I can do it. And I've killed before."

What you don't say is that you would welcome the bullet, but you want to find Cris as badly as he does. You want to save her.

There are two tracking hounds, Mojo and Harley, that have been given Cris's scent from some of her clothes. But you carried her through the woods, her feet never touched the earth, and if there was some residual scent for the dogs to track, that scent, like the chalk marks, has been washed away.

A deputy that Anderson calls Sewell keeps pushing you. Jabbing his finger in your back. He is bully-faced and you can feel his hatred for you.

The dogs are whining and the men are tired and angry. You can feel that they all want an end to this. The dogs want to rend your flesh. The men want to offer you up to their god as a sacrifice. They crave some kind of resolution. Something needs to happen here tonight. Something needs to mark this night for them. And if that thing is your death, then they will just have to settle for that.

DETECTIVE JERNIGAN

The sheriff wanted as many of his deputies in the woods as possible. He had already sent one deputy to the hospital with the missing child's mother, who went into shock after seeing Norris's bedroom. So you volunteered yourself and Burdick to guard the three prisoners— Norris, Dobbs, and the Iranian.

You and Burdick lean against the hood of a sheriff's deputy's cruiser, your backs to Rajaguru who is restrained in the backseat. Your phone rings and you recognize the unique ringtone you've assigned to Mary so that you never miss her calls.

"Hey, how are you?" you say in a low voice. You push off from the car and take your call a few paces away from Burdick. "Did you get any rest? I'm glad for that. I know. We got involved in a local case. Emergency. We should be on our way back within an hour. Two at the most. They needed...The sheriff here... No, I understand. You should call..."

When you glance over to Burdick, to see if he is watching you or trying to listen in, you see that he is over with the prisoners, Norris and Dobbs. Their hands are cuffed behind their backs. He is talking to Norris. You sidle towards them to see what's going on, to hear what's going on. You try to pay attention to Mary and listen to Norris and Burdick at the same time.

"All I want is a cigarette."

"No."

"I appreciate your disposition. The way you feel about me."

"Shut up."

"I would feel the same way. If I were you. If I had committed the crimes you think I did. But I didn't. Truly—"

"Hold on for just a second," you say to Mary. Then to Burdick, "Mike, I wouldn't engage him in conversation. The percussion grenade and everything." You are referencing a recent hostage situation in which the abductor was taken out with a flashbang. As happened here today. The wrinkle was that everything the perpetrator admitted to police was later deemed inadmissible in court because the guy claimed he was suffering from hearing loss when his rights were read to him.

Despite your little heart-to-heart earlier, it looks like Burdick doesn't appreciate you telling him how to do his job. Especially in front of the suspects. Which really was a bad move on your part. To save face, Burdick shows you the back of his hand and continues to engage Norris. If you hadn't been distracted with Mary, you would have pulled your partner aside for the little reminder. Now it's too late. And you have to get back to Mary.

"I don't ask you to believe," Norris says. "Just to...give me the benefit of the doubt until I have—"

"I saw your bedroom," you hear Burdick say.

"Officer, I plead the blood of Jesus. Do you hear me? Those are my children!" Norris gushes like a proud mama. You don't remember him being quite this odd in the past.

"Right. Your children. Do tell." Burdick is deliberately drawing him out now, to goad you.

"You won't be alone tonight," you say to Mary. "I promise." You want to intervene between Norris and Burdick before he takes it too far in making his point, but there is no way you can disengage Mary. She is too emotional. She is in crisis. "I give you my word on that, okay?"

"I don't ask you to believe. Just to consider the possibility. And with that slim possibility firmly in mind, consider that I am only asking for a cigarette. That's all. They're right there in the front seat of that police car where the officer put my belongings."

"If it'll shut you up," Burdick says and turns to retrieve the cigarettes.

"They're Mores. The long ones."

Burdick sticks the smoke in Norris's mouth, and Norris speaks around it, "My lighter is in my pocket here. The other officer missed it when he searched me. This thing has so many little pockets and hidey-holes. Just reach—"

"I've got one. I'm not sticking my hand in your pocket, big boy."

"Indeed not."

You can't believe Burdick is giving Norris a cigarette. That's just stupid. You need to put a stop to it, but Mary is openly weeping, and you can't just say "Gotta go" and hang up. You have to let her finish. In fact, her emotion is so raw that you turn your back on Burdick. It is too personal, too open and real.

Since your back was turned, you do not actually know what happened next, but you can make an educated guess. You imagine that as Burdick cupped the flame and lit the cigarette, Norris brought his knee up into Burdick's groin. There would have been a lot of weight, a lot of force behind that knee. It probably knocked the air out of Burdick, and the pain likely caused him to black out. You don't know if Burdick was stupid enough to have not engaged the thumb break or the safety strap of his holster; nor do you know if the fat man could have possibly been agile enough to squat down and pluck the weapon from Burdick's waist—but both of those things must be true, because what caused you to turn back around was the ear-splitting report of your partner's service weapon discharging.

You drop the phone as you turn. In your mind, you think you can remember hearing it clack on the rocky ground with Mary's lilliputian voice still issuing from it, but of course that can't be true, there is no way you could have heard that. Not in that moment.

Burdick is dead. His brain splattered behind him like a priceless Jackson Pollock. You and Chandler Norris glance at each other over your partner's body as Norris pivots away from you and bends over at the waist. The hem of his housedress rides up enough for him to aim through his stubby splayed legs. You are in his sights. This can't be real. It's not possible. Because a morbidly obese child molester with his hands cuffed behind his back has taken out your partner and gotten the drop on you.

You don't know it, but not long ago he shot and killed a grazing cow from this very position. Investigators will find out it's a sort of party trick he likes to show off.

He fires. He shoots you.

Lying there on the ground, bleeding, you realize that you really can hear Mary's doleful little voice squeaking from the cell phone. So sad, really. Will she ever find peace? Your last thought before the blackness takes you is that you lied to her. Mary will be alone tonight. Maybe every night.

BILLY

"All right," Sheriff Anderson says, "I want you all to spread out. Forget about the supposed chalk marks on the trees. If there were ever any there, we'd have seen one by now. Keep your lights on the ground. Look for any disturbances. Footprints. Overturned leaves. Fresh earth. Jones, try Mojo again. See if there's any kind of scent at all."

You stumble forward. You feel their hatred. You feel your own hatred. You feel the moon hiding itself behind the clouds. You are forsaken.

You keep moving forward. There is nothing else to do. Your trudging feet catch on an exposed root and you stumble. Your feet slip in the wet leafmold, and you land face down in a deep wide puddle. And when you put your hand down to push yourself back up, you feel the garden hose. The air tube.

"This is it," you say, but nobody hears you. You say it again, louder, and one by one, all of the flashlight beams converge on you so that you are lit up like an actor on a stage. You point to the hose so they can see it, and you say, "Here. This is it. Here."

Sewell picks you up by the shirt collar and tosses you aside. He has a shovel and begins turning the earth. It is watery. The spot Chandler chose forms a natural depression in the land. Standing water. Sewell tosses out muddy, watery shovelfuls of dark earth. You think about the X cut into the plastic container's lid, and you imagine water dripping and seeping through it all this time. You think about the garden hose. Was the end of it above the water or below the water? You're not sure. You imagine the hose conducting the pooled water to inside the container. Water gushing inside the sealed tote, filling it in a matter of minutes. A horrible way to die.

Sewell is on his hands and knees. He has uncovered the green plastic lid of the container. He uses his arms to sweep the water off of it, but it's of no use. The water is too deep. He is about to pry the lid off, but Anderson says, "No. See if you can pull it out first."

Deputy Jones gets on the other side and he and Sewell grab the container by the handles, but it doesn't budge. They grunt and strain, but the container does not move. Sewell holds up a hand and both men stop trying.

Sewell takes a new, careful, firm hold of the handles and nods at Jones to do the same. "On three, okay? Ready. One, two, three."

Each man puts every bit of his strength into it, calling on untapped reserves of force, but the container doesn't move. There is nothing. No response. Then, as the officers strain, a deep-throated sucking sound comes from the earth, like a man with pneumonia trying to clear his lungs. The sucking sound grows into a gurgle, and with a boiling intensity, the container is wrested from the begrudging ground.

They set it beside the hole, and Sewell immediately pries off the lid.

The container is full of water. It reminds you of an illuminated swimming pool at night with all the flashlights trained on it. You can see clumpy strands of yellow hair floating like albino seaweed. The back of her fragile head gently bobs like a submerged gourd.

And then—a horrid little exclamation point—you see the butterscotch candy rise to the surface and float there. A tiny sun on a rough sea.

Through the ground-fog, you leave the woods. The flashlights are cast down. Sewell carries Cris's water-logged body, and this bully-faced man is crying.

The rain has long since stopped. The sky is clear. The stars crystalline. There is no moon.

You follow the men across the creek and see the trailer ahead. You are surprised that they have not taken their grief out on you. Or their confusion as to why one group of human beings would do something so vile to another human being—you are surprised that these feelings have not been diverted to violence toward you.

The group approaches the trailer and you hear Sheriff Anderson ask, "What happened to the lights?"

A deputy (you think it is Jones), says. "Generator probably ran out of gas."

"I can hear the damn thing running, so it's not—"

The trailer's floodlights come on and two silhouettes emerge. The gunfire does not go on for very long. And really, it's not very loud, either. A lot of pop pop pop. And when you open your eyes, everybody from the search party is dead. Everybody. It was an ambush against a group of heartsick, spiritually depleted men. It was a slaughter.

"Billy, my boy," Chandler says. "How'd those bread crumbs work out for you?"

Chandler is triumphant, grinning, but then he looks past you and sees Cris still cradled in the fallen Sewell's beefy arms. He goes to her, looks, sniffs, but does not touch her. He leaves her where she rests. And when he looks back up, something is missing from his face. Something is broken.

"Look what you did," he says to you. "Just look."

BILLY

By the time you get to Atlanta, you are very concerned about the environment. Climate change. Greenhouse gasses. PCBs. Mercury contamination. Things of that nature. This is the only world we've got, so it's up to all of us to take care of it. We are stewards of the planet.

At some point in your life, you have to be able to discern between significance and insignificance. What is important and what is unimportant.

Actions and reactions. Responsibility for actions. Significant and insignificant actions. Whether or not we are just specks of dust like some people say we are. How much do you contribute to the end of the world if you throw a soda can out the car window? Or if you dispose of batteries in a landfill? Or if you don't recycle plastics? Or if you kill a little girl?

Chandler is playing one of his tapes. Something to soothe Mama's nerves, he said. *The wheels on the bus go round and round, round and round, round and round.* Frank is reading the early edition of the *Atlanta Journal Constitution.* From the backseat, you lean forward to read it over his shoulder, your feet resting on the Mossberg 500 pump-action shotgun that is stowed on the floorboard there. Chandler decided to drive Frank's Cutlass and leave the sheriff's vehicles and the detectives' sedan. But he gathered up every weapon he could find.

The trunk is full of guns, mace, percussion grenades, and handcuffs. He even found Bessie.

The headline says: KIDNAPPING/MULTIPLE MURDER ROCKS SMALL GA TOWN. And underneath, in smaller type, ENTIRE SHERIFF'S DEPT "WIPED OUT," SAYS LONE SURVIVOR.

Frank tosses the paper in the backseat. "We're fucked."

"Don't be such a sourpuss, Frankie. Didn't I hear you boys say something about Canada?"

"Canada," you echo from the backseat.

"It ain't nothin' but a thing."

"Really?" Frank asks, and there is a tone to his voice that makes you think of how a ten-year-old kid might sound. A sense of wonder, a sense of possibility. A child who is used to swallowing his parents' lies because there is nothing else to eat.

"Of course," Chandler says.

"You really think we could make it?" Frank says, the child who believes with all his heart the promise of Christmas morning.

"Sure. We gotta get rid of this car first thing. If we're driving to the Great White North, we need a better whip than this."

"Where? Let's get it now," the child urges the parent, ready for Christmas to arrive. Then the child snorts a healthy bump of crank from the divot between his calloused knuckles. God bless us everyone.

You are the only one who seems to realize that the direction you're heading is the opposite of north.

You pick up the newspaper, and directly beneath the story about the tragedy in Stockmar County there is another story: SCIENTISTS REPORT OZONE HOLES OVER CANADA AND GREENLAND.

"We'll go shopping, Frankie. Just you nevermind. Hey, Billy-Boy, let Daddy see that paper. Billy? Billy-Boy? Wake up now."

"Huh?"

"Let Daddy see the paper."

You hand it over, and Chandler scans it.

"You boys see that? I'm the mastermind. They'll be setting up check sites. Let's get that new car now. Then get into Atlanta."

"What about Canada?" you ask and cough. Now when you cough, you cover your mouth with a dirty paper napkin. You found a wad of them on the floor-board, under the shotgun. The napkin is spotted with blood. You ball it up and stash it under the seat with the other bloody napkins. You wonder if there is an infection somewhere inside you, because you feel cold one minute and hot the next.

"First we have to get some m-o-n-e-y. Money, honey. We can do that in Atlanta. Then we'll turn our happy asses right around and head north." Still driving and thumbing through the paper, Chandler says, "Listen to this, kiddies. Some sicko is killing people and putting their heads in jars. Maybe I'll send him Uday's head. That lying bastard."

Chandler cackles, rolls down his window, and tosses the newspaper. You turn around and watch the pages separate and tumble in the car's backdraft. And you wonder what kind of impact that will have on the environment. The planet. We are its stewards.

BILLY

The rest stop on Georgia 400 is mostly empty. There is not a lot to it. A squat brick building with bathrooms and vending machines inside. A long-haul rig is parked to one corner of the lot, the driver probably sleeping inside. The faded Cutlass pulls directly up to the structure and parks between a white Chevrolet Equinox and a pristine 1978 caramel-brown Cadillac Eldorado.

A boy of about twelve finishes walking his Chihuahua on the dog path and climbs into the backseat of the Equinox. To you, the little boy is shiny and has a kind of nimbus around him and you remember how the world looked like that to you when you were little and sick with tonsillitis. After a few minutes, the mother, father, and a little girl emerge laughing from the restrooms and join the boy in the car. The father gives the Cutlass and its occupants a disapproving once-over as he backs the SUV out of the parking space. You watch as they merge back on the highway, the white vehicle glowing in your altered vision.

The three of you continue to sit there, not talking. After several more minutes, a big-bellied man in a business suit and a creamy white cowboy hat comes out of the building. He is still drying his hands on a paper towel and his pink face has a look of relief, as though he just took the world's biggest dump. The suit plus the cowboy hat makes you think of Boss Hogg.

Chandler pours himself out of the Cutlass and intercepts the man before he can get to his Eldorado.

"Excuse me, sir?"

Boss Hogg finishes drying the delicate area between his fingers, drops the paper towel in a wire mesh trashcan, and cocks a questioning eyebrow at Chandler.

"I was just wondering," Chandler says, "do you know if, to get to Atlanta, do I need to be on 400 South, or 400 North?

"South," Boss Hogg says, grinning, happy to oblige an idiot who can't find his way to the biggest city in the Southeastern United States. "Just stay on 400 South till you cross 285, you'll hit 85/75, then just follow the signs."

"Thank you so much."

"Sure thing."

The businessman sidesteps Chandler and continues to his car. Chandler waddles forward toward the bathrooms, and then, Columbo-like, he turns around and calls out to the man.

"Oh, sir, uh, just one other thing."

The man pauses, his thumb resting on the chrome push button of the door handle, his eyebrow once again arched, this time in mild irritation. *Need me to draw you a map?*

"Have you ever met Bessie?"

"Bessie?" the business man asks, that eyebrow of his taking on a slant that no longer communicates irritation, only confusion.

Chandler's hand disappears inside the draping crenulations of his garment, his eyes, recessed in their swollen sockets, scan the rest area for witnesses.

"Yes, sir," Chandler nods and brandishes the gun. "Bessie. She speaks only the truth."

Satisfied that no one is around to see or hear, Chandler fires twice in rapid succession. Both bullets strike the man directly in the face, and the shrapnel-like effect of the bone fragments and shattered teeth cause the man's head to more or less explode. Gore spatters the smooth candy-brown hardtop of the Eldorado and Boss Hogg crumples to the ground, dead. Interestingly, the creamy white Stetson tumbles to the pavement about a half second behind its former owner. And it is unscathed. Pure white. No bloodspray or perforation from bone fragments. Just like new. Chandler scoops the hat up and perches it atop his own head. He looks at you and Frank and gestures to the car like a showroom hostess. He looks bright and sparkly to you. Glowing. You are cold.

"Look! It's a Caddie."

In the dream, it's like you are a bird, looking down. You can see the Cadillac making its way down the interstate, the top glittering brown like an insect's back in the midday sun, a Rorschach of dried blood marring its surface. Your birdself wants to swoop down and snatch it with your talons. Eat it. Or maybe feed it to your young.

Chandler's music penetrates the dream, so that even as you soar free through the clean air, it taints you. *Round and round, round and round.* Your birdself soars over lakes, streams, golden fields. A green forest. You see a stream in the forest and glide down to it. There, you see Frank and Chandler and your humanself.

You and Chandler are in the water. He is drowning you, but Frank doesn't see it. Frank is unaware. Frank is on a dry flat rock in the middle of the stream, warmed by the sun. You cry out, but Frank doesn't hear, he doesn't see. And Chandler pushes you deeper and deeper into the cold mountain runoff. He holds you down and you take water into your lungs. You are dead. Drowned. *Beep beep beep, beep beep beep.*

Chandler lets your body go, and the current whisks you away, buoyant, like a plastic milk jug tossed away as trash.

Your birdself watches Chandler pull himself onto the flat river rock and lay down next to Frank. Chandler is pale and obese with rings of fat that make him look like the Michelin Man.

Frank sits up and looks around. And you know it is you that he is looking for. He calls your name three times, and then he jumps into the water. His artificial leg remains on the rock, the not-quite-flesh-colored plastic warming in the sun.

Chandler picks up the leg and it turns into a glass jar. The glass jar holds Mrs. Lovejoy's severed head.

Chandler looks up and he is looking into the eyes of your birdself and he says, "You don't know what an ozone hole is. I'll tell you about Chaos Theory."

Swish swish swish, swish swish swish.

You wake up and feel Frank's palm on your forehead. You hear him say something about a fever, something about a drugstore.

CHANDLER

Kids. It's always something. *Always.*

You ease the Eldorado into the parking lot of an all-night drug store. And you think yet again, *This Eldorado is a really fine automobile.* It floats along like a dream and was built in a time when the comfort of plus-sized people was still of importance. It is *roomy.* Plus, you just like saying the name. The sound of it. *Eldorado.* There is a promise in there. The promise of a promise.

Little Billy has a fever. The poor dear. Always something. Always! What would these children do without you? You are half mama and half daddy and everything that these kids need. You are their protector. That is what these laws out there fail to understand. Yes, you are sick and something inside you is different from what is inside other people, but in the end, what these "officials" will never admit is that you make lives better. You improve the lives of your children. You are their protector. Their steward. In the end, you plead the blood of Jesus, and that is all you can do.

What about the little girl? What about Crisium?

But you are not ready for that thought. You do not yet want to bring that thought to the surface. Not now. Probably never.

You tell Frank to stay in the car with little Billy. Poor Frank. His leg. Hard for him to get around, so you end up doing for him. *See? It really is always something.*

He's like Tiny Tim. Hobbling around. A dirty little street urchin. You love him so. Maybe you should look for a crutch or something. He'd like that. But money is tight. This economy has been tough on everybody. Might have to use a five-finger discount.

You look at your image displayed in an overhead security monitor as you walk through the door. You have really let yourself go. And that diet powder hasn't helped at all. You haven't lost an ounce. Goddamn Uday, that lying bastard. Frank needs to lay off that stuff, too. It's messing up his mind. Giving him pimples. Teenage blemishes. He doesn't even need to lose any weight. Frank has always been svelte.

You grab a little shopping cart and push it forward, but it has a clacking, wobbly wheel and your nerves simply just cannot take that racket, not today, so you put the cart back and select another one, and goddamnit, wouldn't you know it, the second one is worse than the first one. It's always something. Always. You take that cart back and get a third one and that third one is juuuuusssst right.

You head on back toward the pharmacy area and the breeze coming up under your garment feels good after driving for so long. It brings you a little secret pleasure. There is an endcap display of Pajama Jeans and that catches your eye. You've seen them on TV and they look so comfortable. They are pajamas and blue jeans at the same time and whoever thought of that is a genius. You are tempted to get some, but you know they don't have a size big enough to fit you. Most people will never know what it is like to be a big person in a small world. Oh, look, and they have Snuggies. You've seen those on TV, too. They are blankets with sleeves. Another genius idea. Who thinks these things up? They have an XXL. It's in a plaid pattern that you don't really care for, but you toss it in the cart anyway, even though you know the double X isn't going to be big enough, but still, maybe you will lose down enough to fit it, maybe that diet powder will start to work.

On the analgesics aisle, you select a bottle of Bayer aspirin for Billy. Then you see a pink and green box of baby aspirin. That would really be more appropriate, so you get those instead. Plus, they are chewable.

Well, that should do it, so you head on back to the front. Frank doesn't really need a crutch. He gets around just fine. You don't want to be an enabler. You prefer to accent the ability in disability. Yes. Oh, and look, they have baby bottles on sale. Why do those make you think of that little girl? She wasn't a baby. She was getting to be a big girl. And you promised yourself you weren't going to think about that. You were going to put that out of your mind for now. Why dwell? And look at those nursing bottles. A pack of three for $2.99. You can't beat that. That is a steal. And such pretty pastel colors for the nipples. But you don't really need those, do you? Well, there is need, and then there is want, and you most certainly do want these. But should you? Should you really indulge yourself like that? Well, why not? Really, just why the heck not? You deserve it, don't you? You've been under a lot of pressure and need to let off some steam. You put two packs of bottles in your cart. The wipes are on sale, too. And you grab a big can of Enfamil—clinically proven to reduce spit-up—because you don't want to cut corners when it comes to what goes in baby's tummy.

Then you see that they have diapers on sale, too. The price is so low, you'd be a fool to pass up a bargain like that. A nationally recognized brand, to boot. But one part of your mind realizes that they don't make a baby diaper big enough to fit you, and if you are going to keep up this self-deceptive line of thought, you are going to have to make a fully conscious decision to make it work. You will have to go to the aisle where they sell adult diapers, and if you do that, you will be admitting that you are not buying the formula, and the bottles, and the diapers because they are such good deals, you are buying them for other reasons.

Ever since they hooked you up to the bug zapper in Butts County, your mind has been separated into two compartments. There is the Chandler who knows exactly what he is doing, and then there is the Chandler who knows not what he does. That other Chandler takes what he wants, when he wants it. That Chandler does not feel bad about things. That Chandler wants the diapers and he will have them. That Chandler understands that if he gets the diapers and the rest of the paraphernalia, he will have to take care of the cashier on his way out of here—lest she find the morbidly obese customer and his odd assortment of purchases to be unusual, and oh, weren't the police looking for someone who matched that description?

Lying between the Chandler-Who-Knows and the Chandler-Who-Knows-Not is the Middle Ground. And in the Middle Ground a little girl is buried. And you have to jump over that Middle Ground as you travel from *knows* to *knows-not.* So you close your eyes, and you jump.

By the time you make it up to the check-out counter with the baby aspirin, baby bottles, baby wipes, Enfamil powder, and a package of Prevail 3X Bariatric adult diapers, the Chandler who walked in this store, the Chandler whose image was digitally captured by security cameras—that Chandler is gone. Gone with the wind. The Chandler whom you watch put a bullet in the brain of the middle-age woman running the cash register—he is the Chandler-Who-Knows-Not.

From somewhere inside you (perhaps from the electro-convulsive therapy room at Georgia Diagnostic and Classification State Prison in unincorporated Butts County—yes, perhaps that room with the white gurney and beige cloth restraint straps is here inside you), you observe the Chandler-Who-Knows-Not as he reaches over the counter and shoves aside the woman whose body has slumped across the cash register in her sudden death. You watch the Chandler-Who-Knows-Not leave a perfect fingerprint (that will later prove to contain both blood and a bit of brain matter) on the NO SALE button. And as the Chandler-Who-Knows-Not scoops the little bit of cash from the register, he notes with disgust that blood has seeped into the drawer and contaminated the bills. *That will have to be cleaned off,* you hear him think. And then you hear him sigh and mutter under his breath that it's always something. *Always.* And you can't help but to agree.

And you realize that maybe you, the Chandler-Who-Knows, and you, the Chandler-Who-Knows-Not, are not so different after all.

BILLY

When Chandler gets back in the car, he does not speak to you or Frank. When Frank pulls at the bag to look through it, Chandler slaps his hand away. He digs through the bag himself and tosses you a box of baby aspirin. You read the directions on the box and chew up enough of the pills to equal an adult dose.

Chandler gets on the road and stops at the first hotel he comes to. It is, interestingly enough, called Hotel Harvey. He produces a wad of paper money from his muumuu, shoves it at Frank and motions toward the front office. Frank takes the money and counts it. Some of it has blood stains on it. Wet blood stains.

"I can't take this in there. What's wrong with you?"

Chandler reaches back inside the material that drapes him and comes up with a purse-size pack of tissues. He takes the wet money back from Frank and blots it dry. He motions again and Frank goes to get a room.

Chandler has a double bed all to himself. He lies on top of the sheets, naked except for a big white diaper. He is curled up and sucking on his third baby bottle full of chalky-looking formula. The sound of Chandler's lips working the rubber nipple is the only sound in the room. *Phhhhht phhhhht phhhhht phhhht phhhht phhhht.* Over and over and over.

He will not respond to you or Frank. He just stares off into the distance, looking at nothing at all, or maybe something only he can see. You remember that your mother called that pining. When a baby stares at something that is not there, it's called pining.

The most disturbing aspect to all of this is the stride in which Frank is taking it. He does not seem overly concerned. He bumps up every twenty minutes or so and keeps picking at that sore on his face, which looks really, really horrible now. You wonder when will he ever run out of that stuff because you do not like Frank when he uses it and he uses it all the time and he's not really Frank anymore. You might as well be home with Harvey, emptying his pee jug.

There is a wet sound like thick gravy bubbling in a saucepan and then the horrible stench of excrement fills the room. It is overpowering. You can feel it penetrating your hair and clothes. Chandler has shit himself.

Frank squats down next to Chandler's bed and whispers to him, "We've got to keep moving. Chandler, we've got to go. Can you hear me? Chandler, can you hear me? Are you in there? Where are you? Chandler, where are you?"

And Chandler turns over. He speaks, but his eyes remain unfocused. "I'm in the Middle Ground, Frank. The Middle Ground. It's horrible here."

Then his eyes come into focus and he smiles. He reaches down and works off the diaper as best he can. An oil-black smear of feces stains his ass and legs. But he can't get the diaper off by himself and he says, "Help me."

And you do. You and Frank get the diaper off. It

takes almost the whole box of baby wipes to get him clean, but you get him taken care of and wrap the whole mess up in a sheet and put it down the garbage chute. Then, together, the two of you put a clean diaper on Chandler. At least the air in the room is breathable now, even though the odor lingers. Frank fixes a bottle of formula at the sink and puts the nipple to Chandler's lips. He takes the bottle. *Phhhht phhhhht phhhhht phhhht phhhht phhhht.*

After Chandler shot the cowboy businessman, you transferred all of the weapons from Frank's old car to the new one, the Eldorado. Then Chandler went through the man's pockets and found money. He found an iPhone, too, and tossed it to you. "Here little Billy, Daddy got you a video game to play."

The cowboy businessman had been browsing CNN on it. There was a live feed from the ocean floor. A mile under the ocean. It showed the oil bubbling out. Thousands of gallons a minute, just pouring out, poisoning the ocean and nobody could stop it. And you have the phone with you here now, in Hotel Harvey, watching the planet die. You watch that oil blooming like a black flower on the other side of the world. You watch until you fall asleep. And Frank stands over you, guarding you.

When you wake up in the morning, Chandler is sitting in a chair by the window. He looks freshly showered and he's wearing his muumuu. He's browsing one of your travel brochures with theatrical interest. He makes a great show of noticing that you're awake.

"Are you two boys ready to start our vacation?"

And you nod your head, because you are ready.

DETECTIVE JERNIGAN

The lieutenant doesn't want you here, but he understands that you are finding this a little hard to let go. The bullet that Norris fired from Burdick's gun actually grazed your skull. That's how close it was. It etched a new hairline along the right side of your head. Bled like hell, the way scalp wounds usually do, but no real damage. The doctors released you within two hours. Burdick and the five members of the sheriff's department would only be released to the morgue.

Everyone was focusing on Chandler Norris and Frank Dobbs, and dismissing Billy Smith as either a Patty Hearst-type, a quasi-hostage, or a tagalong under Norris's malevolent pied piper spell. But you wanted to know more about the boy.

You tell the lieutenant that Billy Smith met Frank Dobbs at the Shoney's in Marietta where they both worked. Dobbs attacked and brutally injured a coworker, Sidney Edenfield. Billy Smith may have participated in the attack, or he might simply have been an observer. Reports were conflicting. Dobbs and Smith fled the restaurant directly after the assault. They either left together, or Dobbs coerced Smith. Again, witness reports were conflicting. In any case, neither Smith nor Dobbs was seen again until they turned up in Stockmar County. It is also worth noting that Smith's mother died of a rare cancer seven years ago, and his stepfather died in a house fire the same night Edenfield was attacked.

"Was the fire suspicious?" the lieutenant asks.

"Yes and no. Smoking in bed. Blood alcohol, at least what didn't boil off in the fire, was through the roof. Also, the autopsy noted fracturing of the mandible, maxilla, and temporal bones, plus every proximal inter-phalangeal joint on his right hand was broken. All of which could be consistent with the nasty falls drunks are prone to take. Or the results of a bad beating. The kind violent people are prone to administer."

"You're thinking Dobbs."

"I am. Every knuckle on his left hand was broken. Nobody takes a fall like that. And to cast a little more doubt on the drunk-smoking-in-bed theory, Billy Smith was receiving counseling and psychotropic drug therapy for antisocial behavior."

"So he had issues. Hell, my kid takes Ritalin."

"In this case, antisocial is codeword for pyrophilia."

"You mean pyromania?"

"No, *philia*. Pyrophilia. Like a fetish. He gets off on it. Sexual gratification from burning shit. He was starting fires in the school bathroom. Behavior started not long after his mother's death. Also, the counselor's notes hint at suspected abuse by the stepfather. Possibly sexual."

"So the same night a troubled teenage fire bug runs amok and skips town, his abusive stepfather dies in a house fire? Sounds like something out of the Brothers Grimm."

"Yep. But it's still uncertain to what degree Smith was a willing participant in any of this. Don't forget, he was the one leading us to the girl."

"Right. And how did that turn out?"

You don't answer that. Mostly because no answer is expected, but also because a call comes over the lieutenant's phone. The lieutenant tells the caller to hold on, puts it on speaker, and tells the officer on the other end to repeat what he just said.

"A man's body was found on Georgia 400, about sixty miles outside the perimeter. Hidden in a drainage ditch just off a dog trail. Two bullets to the head. The Cutlass was found abandoned at a truck stop five miles away."

"Can they be placed at the scene?"

"No, but a long-haul driver was catching some sleep in the lot. Heard the shots, but didn't get up to investigate."

"The murder victim's vehicle?"

"1978, brown Eldorado hardtop. Fully registered."

"Protocol followed?"

"We've got checkpoints set up all around the perimeter and staggered into South Georgia. They're heading into the city. Or past it. Listen to this, a Walgreens outside Cleveland, Georgia was robbed ninety minutes ago. Cashier shot and killed. Chandler Norris plain as day on the surveillance video. And guess what he stole?"

"I don't care what he stole. They're tracking southerly. Wouldn't they be beyond the city by now?"

"Probably, but since they're hanging out at rest stops and going on shopping sprees, I figured we would look north and south of the perimeter."

"Good. Choppers?"

"Two birds in the sky. Just as soon as dawn breaks."

223

"Good, keep me up to the minute."

"Yes, sir."

"What was it?"

"Sir?"

"What did he steal? Norris."

"Sir, he stole diapers, bottles, formula, wipes. All the shit you need to take care of a baby."

"Are you fucking kidding me? They've abducted an infant?"

"We don't know sir. We have no reports of any child that young missing."

"Reach out to the local communities along their path. We need to know. We've got Kimberly's Call activation, Blue Alert activation. Request a Levi's Call. Contact GEMA. Get their input."

"Yes, sir."

The lieutenant turns to look at you and says, "I've got a Cadillac Eldorado out there tooling around North Georgia with a kidnapped infant, a child pornographer, a violent offender, and a teenage pyro. There is no way this is real. This just can not be real. Where is God?"

FRANK

You are just trying to get from point A to point B. That is all you can do at this time. There is no future. There is no past. There is just point A and point B. And honestly, point B is probably too theoretical to worry about right now, so you take that out of your mind. Fuck that noise. In fact, fuck point A, too. There is no point A. There is no point B. There is just the Middle Ground. That is where Chandler went, and now you are there, too. It feels good. No worries.

Here in the Middle Ground you are pumping gas at five o'clock in the morning at an isolated Exxon station. Here in the Middle Ground you have a lifetime supply of crank, which is good, because you are bumping up every ten minutes now. You haven't slept in what, six days? Something like that. And you are hallucinating. But at least you are aware that you're hallucinating. That's half the battle. At least you understand that the black reticulated python you are fighting against is actually the feed hose of this gas pump. So you are okay. Earlier you were hallucinating that Chandler was wearing a diaper and sucking on a bottle and that he shit his diaper and you and Billy changed him like he was a giant baby. That was pretty fucking vivid.

The python has stopped struggling against you. You have won. You have beat this hallucination and reality swims into view. You look at the digital readout on the gas pump. It is zeros all the way across. What the fuck? Where is the gas? You've been out here a very long time, you finally killed the snake, and there is no gas? Then you see a peeling yellow sticker below the digital display. PAY FIRST AFTER DARK. Fuck. If you're gonna have to go inside, you'll need a bump first. You turn your back to the station and do that very thing. Really, there is no need to turn your back, because you've got the art of discreet bump down to a science. You could bump up in a crowded elevator and no one would be the wiser. They might think you rubbed your nose was all. Still, you turn your back. Best to play it safe.

You step up to Chandler's window and tell him you need cash. He gives you a fifty. Billy is in the backseat playing with that video game thing. He's got it plugged into the cigarette lighter and the light from the screen flickers across his face. He's playing some kind of undersea adventure game. Looks like he's having fun. In a way, this really is like being on vacation.

Inside, the bright florescent lights hurt your eyes. You walk around the store a little bit, thinking maybe you'll get something to eat. You haven't eaten in a long, long time. But you're not hungry. You pick up a donut with white icing that's sealed in plastic. They pump these things with chemicals to keep them shelf stable. You read that somewhere. The white icing looks like pus. Like something you would squeeze out of a zit. You put it back down. There is one of those curved mirrors right above your head and you can see the counter girl looking at you. Watching you. Then you look at yourself. Scraggly beard, dark circles under your eyes. Face tats. Skin like dough. Like the icing on that fucking donut. The red inflamed meth sore on your cheek stands out in sharp contrast. It takes every tiny little bit of self-control you have left to keep your hands at your sides. To not pick at the sore. You want to pick at it, to doctor it, so very bad. And your eyes are glassy and blown like you had a fucking stroke or something. You look away. You feel angry. Like you want to kill someone. Like you want to shatter someone's face. Like you want to smash that goddamn mirror and grind the girl's face in it. Yep. Yank everything off the shelves. Shatter glass. Throw bottles. Kick shit. And the cashier would be screaming. Screaming. Just fucking screaming. You would grab that bitch and drag her to the stockroom and you would rip her fucking clothes right the fuck off her and she couldn't stop you couldn't stop you couldn't stop you and you would put her face down on the dirty floor and you would rape her rape her rape her rape her rape rape rape.

Maybe some coffee. No, you don't like coffee. Maybe a Diet Coke. And then you remember you are out of cigarettes. You haven't smoked one in a long time, but you've barely noticed. You just keep bumping up. This could be like a cure for smoking. You wonder if doctors are aware of this. Many thousands of lives could be saved. Then you see a display of Tahitian Treat in old-fashioned glass bottles and you didn't realize they even made that shit anymore. Fuck yeah. You grab one. It's warm, but fuck it.

The girl is looking at you. Is she flirting? You smile at her. Your crooked little half smile that you practice in the mirror. It's pretty cute.

At the counter you say, "Pack of Marlboro, reds."

Normally you smoke Marlboro Lights, but for some reason you want to impress the girl, so you go for the real deal. And why is she looking at you like that? You throw the fifty on the counter and say, "The rest in gas." And she pulls out one of those pen things and starts scribbling on the bill and you guess she doesn't trust you, and you think to yourself that you'll show that whore what trust is and you realize that sounds like something Chandler would say. And you think about that for a minute, and when you come out of the thought, the girl is gone. Disappeared. Then you look down and there she is behind the counter. And you can't tell which is a brighter red, her blood or the Tahitian Treat that sprayed everywhere when the bottle shattered against her skull. You must have hit her after all. You lean over the counter and pull the cigarette rack down and pluck out a deck of Marlboro Lights, hard pack. The reds hurt your throat after a while.

BILLY

Your fever is back. You are shivering. You sit in the backseat with your feet propped on the Mossberg shotgun that lies on the floorboard. You hold Boss Hogg's iPhone in your hands and watch the live video feed from the ocean floor on the other side of the globe. 750,000 barrels of oil per day. Just spewing out of a crack in the earth's plates. There is no one there to hear it. Just a silent ejaculation that will never stop until the ocean is poisoned, the food chain wrecked, life as we know it gone forever.

Every time you look up, you see the back of Frank's fist leaving his nose. Chandler is humming. *Round and Round. Round and Round.*

Dawn has broken and the growing light hurts your eyes. The Eldorado is hurtling at seventy-five miles per hour down I-85 South toward Atlanta. South is the opposite direction of Canada. You get what you deserve.

Every once in a while, the car passes under one of those lighted dynamic message signs that give out traffic information in massive glowing yellow letters. Usually the signs tell how many minutes to the next exit, or if there is a closed lane or something. Now the signs are about you:

AMBER ALERT/LEVI'S CALL
KIDNAPPED CHILD
TUNE TO RADIO/TV

You notice that they just updated the signs to include the Cadillac, its color, and license plate.

But there are more important things. You watch the oil boil out of the earth. It never stops. Never stops. It is silent at the bottom of the ocean. A mile underwater, you can hear your own heartbeat. Like now, silence, just the sound of your heart. You can even feel it. *Thwump-thump. Thwump-thump.* In your throat you can feel it, and you swallow it back, but that doesn't work because you can still feel it and hear it even louder now and that makes you think about that story you read in Ms. Wiggins' English class about the guy who went crazy after he killed his boss and hid the body under the floor. But he could still hear the heart beating, just like you can now hear your own heart beating, and maybe it's not even your own heart you hear. Maybe it is Cris's. Maybe you are crazy now. And your heart speeds up into one continuous *thump-thump-thwump-thumpthwumpthump thumpthumpthumpthumpthump.*

You see Chandler and Frank are both craning their necks to look out the window and up into the sky, and so you do too. And there is a helicopter up there. Over you. Following you. Like the moon used to do. Before it forsook you. *Thwumpthwumpthwumpthwumpthwump thwump.* And then there is another one. Two. Two helicopters following you. *Thumpthumpthumpthump.* You do not need to test it. You do not need to look away and time it and then look back later. Because they will still be there. They really are following you. You know this. Those helicopters are going to be with you from here on out, their rotors pulsing reminders of the crime you committed.

You hear sirens in the distance, reaching out for you. Growing closer. Chandler adjusts the rearview mirror to get a better look, and his eyes are looking directly into your eyes when he says, "Well, boys and girls, looks like we're fucked."

And then Frank mumbles something and Chandler says, "How's that again, Frankie?"

"Stardust," Frank says. "Billion-year-old carbon."

"Yep, it's always something," Chandler says and floors the gas pedal. The uptick in acceleration nudges you backward. "I'll show those motherfuckers just exactly what stardust is."

And on the screen in your hands, the black oil jets and bubbles in silent toxic fury a mile underwater. It never stops. A thousand gallons every time you blink your eyes. The earth is wounded, cracked open, bleeding out like the victim of a drive-by shooting.

The sirens surround you now, the helicopters thumping and sucking the air out of the car. The interstate has widened to six massive lanes, like veins that carry blood to the heart. And you and Frank and Chandler are like a virus, a pollution in the blood, and that makes you think of a poem but you can't remember it exactly, and in the distance, you can see the I-285 interchange. Criss-crossed ribbons of elevated asphalt that hug the city of Atlanta, holding it in. And at the base, a mass of vehicles. Police cruisers. Emergency responders, vans, hummers. A mass of metal set to stop you.

Chandler does not ease up on the gas. The speed-ometer is buried past 120. You look at the undersea oil spill. The environmental catastrophe. You look up when you feel the car decelerate. You see that Frank is holding Chandler's right leg. Lifting it off the gas pedal. The Eldorado coasts down to a crawl. The flotilla of police cars behind you has slowed as well. They are keeping their distance.

Frank turns to you and says, "Get out."

You are frozen. You don't know what to do. But you don't have to think. Frank thinks for you. You have always been with Frank—carbon commingling amongst the stars. He leans over the seat and opens the back door. He picks up the Mossberg and uses it to poke you, to prod you. He pushes you out of the car, and you land roughly on the six lanes of asphalt of I-85. You tumble. You bang your head, your elbow, your knee. But you are okay.

You get to your feet. You want back inside. Back with Frank. But you are too late. Tires squeal. The Eldorado takes off. The rear door slams shut from the force. You are alone. Then the police are there. You put your hands over your head, and you are surrounded by uniformed City of Atlanta police officers. A distorted, amplified voice is yelling "Down on the ground! Down on the ground!" So you drop. And there is a violent knee on your back, pinning you like a bug, your wrists bound with brutal force and another voice asks, "Is the infant safe?"

FRANK

Stars.

My God, the stars.

It's full of stars.

That is what you think as you force Chandler's sausage-like leg down on the gas pedal. The acceleration forces your body back against the seat. You can't see the speedometer, so you judge the car's speed by how the stars slide past you. Feels like the speed of light. The stars are just streaks of white. It's like you are James T. Kirk and you just gave the order to engage warp drive.

Stars. Everywhere stars.

And you feel the shotgun in your lap. And you pick it up. You feel for the trigger, because you cannot see it. All you can see is stars. *My God, the stars.* You thumb the safety and put your finger around the trigger.

You are blind, and you say, "Daddy? Are you there, Daddy?"

"I'm right here, Frankie."

"Where?"

"Here, Frankie. I'm right here. The Middle Ground. I'm in the Middle Ground."

And yes, that's right. That is where you are. The Middle Ground. And it is full of stars. My God, the stars.

And you think, *Fire every single gun you've got and explode right into outer space.*

233

You aim where Chandler's head should be. You hear him crying out, but the cry is cut short. The shotgun going off in the car's interior is like a star exploding. Supernova.

The driver's side window evaporates in what must be a red smear of glass and blood, and the Cadillac's interior decompresses like a pressure breach in orbit. You do not see Chandler's headless torso slump across the steering wheel because you see only stars. My God, the stars. Immediately, you feel the car jerk to the right. You hear the tires squeal, then a solid jolt and for a moment, nothing, just peace, and then violent impact, the car is rolling. You feel something tug at your arm, and you realize your arm was just pulled off, severed. That's what people who have their leg bit off by a shark say. It felt like a tug.

There are more tugs. Then something hard punches at your throat and the blood is warm, like a bath. No pain. You might already be dead, just your brain keeps working a little bit. And then the fire.

You are golden.

BILLY

From the back of the police car, looking forward through the wire screen partition, you watch the Eldorado roll and catch fire. This backseat smells of your fear, and the fear of a thousand other bad people.

Police cruisers and ambulances approach the fiery remains from both sides. They approach with caution. And you are right there with them. It is slow motion. You are drawn to the fire. It soothes you. Makes you feel better. Makes the fear smell not so strong. And despite everything, you feel a hardness in your pants.

Off to the left, something catches your eye. A small dense plume of black smoke rises from an otherwise empty piece of highway. Something thrown from the car.

The police car inches forward, and the small burning thing comes into focus. It's a leg. Frank's plastic leg. On fire. Melting. Bubbling. Oily black smoke wafts from it, polluting the atmosphere. And you have one final thought before you cum. That poem you were trying to remember comes back to you. Again, from Ms. Wiggins's English class. You can't remember who the poet was, but you remember the words.

Is this God?
Where, then, is hell?
Show me some bastard mushroom
Sprung from a pollution of blood.
It is better.

BILLY

There have been many interviews. They feed the court of public opinion, your lawyer says. You have a good lawyer. At first you had a public defender who was maybe not so good, but then a fund was started in your name. The Billy Smith Defense Fund. It was kind of like the fund that Kroger and the First Baptist Church of Christ took up for your mother when she was sick. You have had visitors who are famous and who have given you money. Eddie Vedder. Sean Penn. George Clooney. They said they believed you were innocent and that this was a travesty of justice. There were commercials and articles and stuff in the newspapers. They said that just like Cris and the woman from Walgreens and the girl from the Exxon station and all those dead deputies, you were a victim of Chandler and Frank—and don't forget Harvey, he was a victim, too.

In the end, you were acquitted of the murder charges and Taylor Swift was at the trial and she wrote a song about it.

You have so much money left in your defense fund that you could easily fly first class to Canada. But you don't want to do that. You want to use the Greyhound travel voucher that Mrs. Lovejoy has sent you. You were able to get your passport while you were still at the Grierson not-a-prison holding and processing facility. Brad Pitt helped with that.

The documentary film woman with the razor blade earrings and tattoos (but not like Frank's) and the anarchy motorcycle helmet offers to take you to the bus station. You ride on the back of the bike with your arms around her middle. The open air feels good.

She films you walking onto the loading platform holding just a plastic grocery bag with your few belongings. There is a bank card in there with direct access to your defense fund. You have plenty of money. Maybe you will buy a case of Natural Light beer, in loving memory of Harvey.

She keeps the camera on you as you climb the three steps onto the bus. You take a window seat by yourself and when you look out the window she is still out there filming you. You look away because you've heard that you're not supposed to look directly into the camera except this is a documentary and of course it's okay in documentaries. You've told your whole story to that camera. Still, it's time to look away from it. It will be like a made-up movie now, not real, like you are Jon Voight and this is the end of *Midnight Cowboy*, only Dustin Hoffman (Frank) died before he got on the bus. Fade to black.

The bus rolls, chewing up mile after mile, and you sit there staring out the window for what feels like hours. You do not move. You are scared to move because this feels like a dream, and you are afraid that if you move this new reality will just evaporate. That it will be lost to you forever. Is this what you deserve? Have you earned this ending? Or is it another ending that you deserve? If you do not move, maybe you won't have to find out.

But of course, eventually, you have to move. You can not stay frozen. You need to experience this new reality, test it out. But no, you are still too afraid.

The scenery drags past, and gets greener. The sun sets, and then, there is the moon. Is it following you? Yes, you are pretty sure the moon is following you. You are almost certain of it. And that makes you believe. You believe that this is real.

You remember the day that the detective came to talk to you at the holding facility. Jernigan. It felt like he was absorbing you with his eyes.

He had a picture of a little girl, and he handed it to you.

"You never saw her before? He never mentioned her name?"

"What was her name?"

"Emily."

"Emily. No."

And that was it. He left. You never saw him again.

You take the St. Christopher medallion from around your neck. It was in the envelope with the bus ticket. At the bottom. From Mrs. Lovejoy. No note. You do not know what it means. Why she returned the medal to you. It could mean that she wants you to wear it around your neck as a reminder of what you did. So you never forget. Not even for a second. So you never have a moment of peace.

Or it could mean that she absolves you. That you are forgiven.

You hold the necklace with the chain draped and looped through your fingers, and moonlight glints off as it sways. You enjoy the heft of it. The realness of it. St. Christopher is the patron saint of travelers. He protects them. But that is a lie. That is not real. That lie has been proven. You did much reading in the not-a-prison, and you know that Christopher helped people to safely cross a treacherous river that had taken the lives of many travelers. Eventually, a small child asked Christopher to carry him across the dangerous river. Crossing the violent water, Christopher found the child to be unbearably heavy. And Christopher almost succumbed to the weight and let the child perish. But he didn't. He carried the child safely to the other side. And the child told Christopher that he was so heavy because he was Christ The King, carrying the world's burdens on his shoulders.

Where was St. Christopher when you carried a child on your back? Why did he let the river sweep her away?

The slinky chain slips through your fingers, and the medallion falls into the crevice between the seat and the seat back. You dig your fingers in there, hoping to fish it out, but what you find is a butane lighter wedged in the crack. It's green. A Cricket. You hold it up to the overhead light and through the semi-translucent plastic you can see that the fuel reservoir is three-quarters full. There is a tightening in your pants. A weight. A pleasant heft. A substance. You are substantial. You are real. You hold the lighter down low and spin the wheel across the flint and a yellow-orange flame spurts up. And you are hard. Rock fucking hard. It has been so long.

You look behind you, down the aisle, and notice that the bus has a bathroom at the back. The little red card in the door reads OCCUPIED/OCCUPADO, and it slides back to green and the door opens and a Mexican boy with big dark eyes comes out.

You get up and make your way down the aisle, holding your hands in front of your crotch because you are a man of weight and substance.

You are real. You are there.

You open the bathroom door and hear the little red card snick into place as you close it, and you are swallowing in anticipation. Swallowing, swallowing, swallowing.

It is a pleasure to burn.

When you emerge from the bathroom and return to your seat, you feel better. You stare straight forward. Because this is the test. This is the test on which all else depends. And you want to ready yourself for it. Steel yourself against the possible results. And finally, when you are ready, you look out the window and you have to swallow back your emotions because you understand now that everything is going to be okay. You are okay. You are forgiven. You know this because you are special. Because the moon is still there. Following you. The moon is following you.

You swallow.

You are forgiven.

But it may be asked, where can a subject end? It goes without saying that divisions are more or less arbitrary, if we are seeking reality, for things are together, and the more we look into the world the more we find it to be an organic mechanism of absolute relativity.

THE DOCTOR

Wednesday. The day you have been dreading.

You get up just like it is any other day. Cheryl has the coffee ready when you get downstairs. The Starbucks half-caf that you like so much. You have reached that point in middle age where you have to watch your caffeine intake. Salt. Sunlight. Shit like that.

You eat half a grapefruit with your coffee. It tastes like crapola.

Cheryl kisses you goodbye. She knows it is a bad day for you (and a worse day for someone else—ha-ha) but she knows you well enough to not ask if you are okay or to try and say something stupid like, what you are going to do tonight is really a humane thing and you are performing a service for the community and she is proud of you yadda yadda yadda, ad nauseam. But she will not say that. Partly because she is smarter than that, but mostly because both of you know that this little part-time job of yours is most certainly not something you are doing for the good of the community. It's simply a way to make extra money because both of you want to go to Paris for your twentieth wedding anniversary, but you don't want to dip into your retirement accounts to do so. There is an extra-tasty cabin on Lake Tahoe that you both see yourselves in ten years from now and neither of you wants to jeopardize that. So, you got yourself a sweet little part-time job to bankroll the Paris jaunt.

Irregular, erratic hours, but the pay is good.

The morning is cool, so you leave the car windows up as you drive in to the office. With the car closed up, you can smell yourself. You smell like a doctor. You smell dry and dusty—like white birch tongue depressors—and sharp—like isopropyl alcohol.

It is a usual day for you. You see the same old shit that you have seen every day since you and Bob Zegna opened an internal medicine practice together. Ingrown toenails, broken fingers, infected piercings, generalized anxiety, persistent headaches, kids with fevers, men with limp dicks, women with dry pussies.

You get back home at four. Cheryl is out somewhere, but she has left dinner for you in the microwave. Eggplant parmesan. You zap it for seventy seconds. It is good.

You get to the prison at six o'clock. Thank God there are no protestors. Not yet, anyway. You hate, hate, hate protestors, and this one has been getting a lot of play in the media. CNN, Fox, the networks, the bloggers, the Twitterers, the YouTubers. Mostly because the condemned, just barely an adult when sentenced, had been diagnosed with possible learning disabilities and some definite mental health issues when he committed his crimes, and because Billy Smith is the only person in America on death row who has not been convicted of murder. Smith was convicted of Kidnapping With Bodily Injury—a capital crime in the Peach State. The talking heads like to bat it back and forth how capital punishment, if used at all, should be reserved only for those who took another human being's life. The other side likes to point out how Crisium Lovejoy did indeed lose

her life even if Billy Smith was not specifically charged—
and let's not forget the various other persons who lost
their lives along the way. And also there was the conten-
tion that Smith was in fact a kidnap victim himself,
abducted by Norris and Dobbs. That it was a Patty
Hearst scenario. A Stockholm Syndrome situation.

But you try not to concern yourself with the politics
of it. What would be the point? You are not Eddie
Vedder. And Billy Smith is not Troy Davis. (And Christ
a'mighty what a fuckup that was. News vans and
swelling crowds out here while you had Davis inside,
strapped to the gurney, waiting for the Justices of the
United States Supreme Court to finish texting and
Skyping each other and make up their ever-loving minds
whether Davis should live or die. And in the end, it was
you in the death room with him. It was you who had to
say, in essence, *Well, Troy, old pal, thanks for playing,
but it looks like Caesar has given you the thumbs down.
Better luck next time.* What a fucked-up night.)

So you are glad that you do not have to cross a
protest line or brave the probing lens of the media as you
drive through the gate. Georgia Diagnostic and Classification Prison is about an hour outside of Atlanta, and
apparently nobody felt compelled to make the commute
from the city to hold a candlelight vigil. Of course, now
that they were scheduling the executions at seven p.m.
instead of midnight, candlelight vigils lost some of their
impact. It's still daylight outside, for Christ's sake.

You walk through the prison yard to the Death
House. There is only one entrance. When you walk in,
you have to cross through the observation room where
there are three wooden benches as long as church pews

that face a glass window obscured by drawn curtains. Almost like a little movie theatre. Everything except a popcorn machine.

A small door to the left of the observation window leads to the execution chamber. You enter. The execution chamber smells the same way you do—dry, like dusty tongue depressors and sharp, like alcohol. The walls are cinderblock, painted an antiseptic white. The door that leads to the death watch cell is painted a cheery lemon yellow. You realize that is absurd, but it's true. It's a cheerful lemon color. The door's trim is black, and the baseboards are black. White curtains cover the observation window. The gurney is covered with a black pad, black pillow, and black restraining straps that dangle over the sides. It's all really quite color coordinated. The extensions that support the condemned man's arms are black, too. They jut off from the gurney like the wings of an ebony angel.

There are two metal ports in the wall directly behind the gurney and that is what interests you most at this particular point in the evening. You walk through the lemon-yellow door and avert your eyes from the death-watch cell and the two correctional officers standing guard there. You turn left into the room directly behind the death chamber and find Warden Clark Jerrod. He is talking to the nurse on duty. You nod and exchange a few words, but really you can't stand Jerrod. Arrogant prick.

You busy yourself with running lines from two saline drips to the wall ports. One line will run pure saline only. The other line, the hot one, will run saline and a pertinent other drug. You affix a tubing manifold to the hot line. And to this manifold you attach three plunger apparatuses that feed into the line. Two of these plungers you fill with harmless saline solution, and the third you load with 120 milliequivalents of potassium chloride, a salt which is essential for the proper health of human beings, but in this instance will be delivered as a massive overdose that will stop a human heart like a sledge hammer.

Hmmmm. You wonder how you say potassium chloride in French. And are you really killing people to finance a Parisian vacation? Can that really be true? No, of course that is not true. You will not be the person who depresses the plunger, the one that delivers the lethal overdose to Billy Smith's veins. No, all you are going to do is set it up for the executioners. You are not the executioner. The three men who depress those plungers will have to sort out their consciences on their own. The reason for the three separate plungers is so that no individual will have to bear the burden of knowing he or she delivered the hot dose. So those anonymous prison personnel will go home tonight knowing that there is a one-in-three chance that they took the life of a fellow human being in the course of their work. But were those odds really skewed enough to help a man sleep at night? Personally, you don't see the point in the three-card-monte ruse, because in the im-mortal words of Meat Loaf, two out of three ain't bad. Ha-ha. If it helps them sleep at night, then fine.

And what helps *you* sleep at night? The fact that there is a zero-out-of-three chance that you delivered the lethal dose? Well, yes, actually, that is exactly what helps you sleep at night. And in any case, what's the point of this line of thought? There is no point to it. So stop thinking it. Yours is not to reason why, yours is to watch 'em die. Ha-ha. Another good one. You are on a roll, my friend. The bons mots are just a rollin' 'round your noggin. And besides, it's not like you're in here every week overseeing an execution. Good God, no. You've been doing this a little over a year now, and this is only the fifth execution in all that time. But you get a check every month all the same. And those checks are adding up nicely. How are they gonna keep you down on the farm after you've seen Paree? Ha-ha.

When you walk back into the death chamber, the nurse and the correctional officers have Billy Smith strapped to the gurney. You are surprised at how old he looks, he was just a kid in the photos you've seen, but you realize that the appeals process can drag on for years, decades even.

The nurse has run the wall lines to the peripheral venous access that she has prepared in each of his arms. You inspect her work, and you are satisfied with the place-ment of the IV catheters. The saline seems to be flowing just fine. Smith looks you in the eyes and you nod to him, pat his shoulder. You switch on the high-intensity LED surgical light that hangs over the gurney from a mechanical arm. The bright warm light is not needed, but the intensity of it causes Billy Smith to close his eyes against it. And that is why you turned it on. You can't look into their eyes. You just can't. It's too much.

Two correctional officers stand at the ready, but Billy Smith is strapped down tight. He is not going to move.

"In just a minute I'm going to give you something to relax."

You turn your back on him and prepare a syringe with two hundred milligrams of pentobarbital to induce relaxation and unconsciousness. This dosage does not approach a lethal level and is therefore not in violation of your Hippocratic Oath. Nope, you're A-Okay. You are cool on Christ. It's all good, brutha'.

You look at the clock and you've timed it just right. It's time. No standing around making chit-chat with the condemned, making small talk, telling him how you're just picking up some extra hours because the missus wants to see the Eiffel Tower and you know how women are, wink-wink. You are not here to offer counsel or words of wisdom. That's not your job. The chaplain took care of that already.

The white curtains go back and it's showtime. The warden steps out and gives his little speech about this and that and the Superior Court of the State of Georgia, introduction of lethal chemical into your bloodstream, until such time, et cetera, et cetera, et cetera, and he wraps it all up with how the little special phone didn't ring so he reckons the Georgia State Board of Pardons and Paroles in Atlanta has not decided to grant clemency. *Tough titty, said the kitty.*

The warden gives you the nod and you stab the hypodermic into the right side catheter and you put your hand back on the inmate's shoulder while you're doing it. *Tough titty, said the kitty, but the milk sure was good.*

You and the nurse watch together. When you've both deemed the prisoner to be unconscious, you will give the warden another nod, and he will signal to the men on the other side of the wall to let loose with those chemicals the state of Georgia has seen fit with which to kill a man in the most humane way possible.

You watch as Billy Smith's eyes close. Movement below the prisoner's waist draws your attention and sure enough Billy Smith is sporting a hard-on. Not a bad way to ease on out of this world. You and the nurse share an amused glance. You'll have to note it in your write-up. *Tumescence of the penis observed after administration of pentobarbital.* Then you see his Adam's apple moving. Up and down. Up and down. He is swallowing. Over and over, he is swallowing. This does not alarm you, because you have seen this before. It's a common side effect of the pentobarbital. Never had that problem with the sodium pentothal, but there was that big brouhaha about how it was perhaps improperly imported into the states and whether it was effective anyway, so now they use the pentobarbital and it works fine with just this one weird side effect. The swallowing goes on for two minutes. Then it stops. Billy Smith is clearly unconscious.

Next you load the catheter with fifty milligrams of pancuronium bromide, a curare mimetic which will paralyze the patient. This is procedure. Don't want to take the chance of any unseemly muscle tremors upsetting the observers. Once administered, you rake a tongue depressor up and down the soles of both feet and get no reaction, the nurse silently concurs and you give the warden the nod. And in the room behind you, the lethal drug begins to inch its way through IV tubing, into this room, and into Billy Smith's veins.

You wait.

And then the worst thing that could possibly happen

actually does happen. Something that is simply not possible. The inmate shows signs of consciousness. Billy Smith speaks. It is just a faint whisper, but you see his lips move and there is an observation room full of journalists and the mother of the kidnapping victim watching this and you could damn well lose your license over a fuckup of this magnitude—goodbye medical career, goodbye part-time job, and goodbye gay Paree. But these are a human being's last words, and they deserve to be heard. It is your job to hear them. To witness. So you lean over Billy Smith. You put your ear to his lips and your fingers to his carotid artery like you are just checking for a pulse even though he is hooked up to a heart monitor and you damn well know the lethal overdose hasn't reached his veins yet. It's like maybe you decided you don't trust that rickety old heart monitor and your stethoscope just wasn't good enough for a job of this magnitude. So you have your fingers to his throat and your ear to his lips like it's the seventeenth fucking century and you're trying to rule out catalepsy. Like maybe Edgar Allen Poe is making this shit up on the fly. And who knows, maybe Poe really is writing this, because goddamnit, past all reason, Billy Smith whispers again. He's supposed to be paralyzed and unconscious, not horny and chatty. How is this even possible? You'll write it up in your notes as a facial tic. A muscular tremor. The nurse won't say anything. Her job is on the line, too. Only it wasn't a tic. Billy Smith spoke. And you heard him. You understood him.

And then the pulse in his neck is gone. Just stopped. Like his heart has finally been hit by that proverbial sledgehammer. He is dead.

By order of the state of Georgia, a condemned man's last words are to be preserved. Written down and recorded. Issued to the media. Them's the rules. But you can't admit the possibility that you fucked up. There is law, and there is man's moral law. There is right and there is wrong. And then there is Paris. And we'll always have Paris. You'll keep these words to yourself. In fact, maybe you misunderstood. Because what he said really didn't make any sense. You must have misunderstood. No, no you clearly heard his last words. Your ear is still damp from the two puffs of fetid air on which those meaningless syllables arrived.

Just two words.

The moon.

EXTRACTS

(139) Human beings may be classified, in a general way, into normal and abnormal. By "abnormal" is meant departure from the normal. While the term "abnormal" often suggests ethical or aesthetical characteristics, it is here employed with no such reference. Thus a great reformer and a great criminal are both abnormal in the sense of diverging much from the average or normal man. The principal and extreme forms of human abnormality are insanity, genius, and crime. The third form, "crime," includes all excessive degrees of wrong.

(8) The present work may perhaps be considered as an introduction to abnormality in general, giving a description, diagnosis, and synthesis of human abnormalities, which seem to be constant factors in society.

(7) While certain forms of abnormality as genius and talent are desirable, the larger number, such as criminality, pauperism, insanity, etc., are not.

(44) The criminal by nature has a feeble cranial capacity, a heavy and developed jaw, a large orbital capacity, projecting superciliary ridges, an abnormal and symmetrical cranium, a scanty beard or none, but abundant hair, projecting ears, frequently a crooked or flat nose.

255

(44) Criminals are subject to Daltonism; left-handedness is common; their muscular force is feeble. Alcoholic and epileptical degeneration exists in a large number. Their nerve centers are frequently pigmented. They blush with difficulty. Their moral degeneration corresponds with their physical, their criminal tendencies are manifested in infancy by onanism, cruelty, inclination to steal, excessive vanity, impulsive character.

(44) The criminal by nature is lazy, debauched, cowardly, not susceptible to remorse, without foresight; fond of tattooing; his handwriting is peculiar, signature complicated and adorned with flourishes; his slang is widely diffused, abbreviated, and full of archaisms.

(50) The deformations of the genital parts have a special diagnostic value, because a part of them in both sexes leads to sexual disorders of every nature, which are causes of mental troubles. The most frequent deformations are: atrophy of the testicles, phimosis, stunted or deformed penis; fissure forms of the urethra, growing together of the penis with the scrotum, hypertrophy of the clitoris, [and] closing of the back part of the vagina. See: (31) Criminal teratology [pathological sexuality, onanism, pederasty, sodomy, masochism and sadism, and saphism.]

(9) An individual may be said to be abnormal when his mental or emotional characteristics are so divergent from those of the ordinary person as to produce a pronounced moral or intellectual deviation or defect.

(31) The study of the criminal can also be the study of a normal man; for most criminals are so by occasion or accident and differ in no essential respect from other men.

(9) The normal class of individuals, who greatly exceed all other classes in number; these in every community constitute the conservative and trustworthy element and may be said to be the backbone of the race.

(189) We do not feel because we do not know. In our ignorance we allow ourselves to believe that the criminal is merely a victim of ancestry and of surroundings; that he is forced to this life of crime by an inexorable necessity; that criminality is a disease, perhaps transmitted, perhaps contracted; that the criminal is not guilty but only unfortunate; that he is not an object of condemnation but only of commiseration. Every man is the resultant of three factors—his ancestors, his surroundings, and his individuality. No man can be forced into crime.

(190) The responsibility of the criminal must be divided among these factors. It is one of the most tremendous facts in human life that, for every action, every impulse, every thought, every temptation resisted or victorious, we are fastening not only ourselves but those who may come after us in remote generations.

(42) The individual study of the criminal and crime is a necessity if we are to be protected from ex-convicts, the

most costly and the most dangerous class we have. But the criminal can not be studied without being seen and examined.

(41) If a nerve of a normal organism is cut, the organs in which the irregularities are produced are those which the nerve controls. In this way the office of a nerve in the normal state may be discovered. The criminal is, so to speak, the severed nerve of society, and the study of him is a practical way (though indirect) of studying normal men. And since the criminal is seven-eighths like other men, such a study is, in addition, a direct inquiry into normal humanity.

(41) Crime can be said, in a certain sense, to be nature's experiment on humanity.

(52) Insanity is the involuntary blindness of the mind by the passions, which inspire false ideas; but its essence is the absence of moral opposition, of reason, and of light, clarifying the mind.

(201) Insanity, as well as that form of aberration which is called criminality, is not possible with a normal brain.

(201) The anomalies of the hemispheres are either arrests of developments or acquired alterations. The first are all prenatal, the latter are either contracted before birth, during birth, or during life. See: (238) Insanity, Idiocy, Imbecility, Cretinism, Feeble-mindedness, etc.,

and (271) Morphinism, Opium habit, Chloralism; Ether, hashish, or cocaine mania.

(31) Criminal hypnology concerns those hypnotic and partially hypnotic conditions in which crime is committed.

(44) Nature is responsible for the born criminal, society (in a great measure) for the criminal by occasion.

(44) If punishment rests on free will, the worst men, the criminals by nature, should have a very light punishment or none.

(190) There are three ways in which we may deal with a bad man. In the first place, we may get rid of him altogether by death or exile.

(45) One class of criminals are those with regressive, arrested moral development, innate criminals; for these society has but one remedy, elimination.

(191) A bad man can be and ought to be made a good man by the very process which may also at once appease popular indignation caused by his behavior, and strengthen others when tempted to imitate him. This can not be applied to all men. There are some whom no form of penal discipline will ever make estimable or useful, or even harmless.

(163) Ethics in the widest sense of the term means regulation of action; in the more definite sense it represents those duties which must be performed in the interest of society.

(200) Dr. Jacobi, of New York, spoke on brain crime and capital punishment: the composing parts of the brain must have been developed simultaneously and equally; essential organs and functions, particularly reasoning power and will, must not be disturbed... however great the number of hitherto unrecognized anomalies in the brain will become in the future, they will belong to two large classes, such as inflammation and humors. To these two classes belong the local disorders which have been found in the brains of criminals. They have been denominated criminal brains. The constitutional criminal is a tainted individual, and has the same relation to crime as the epileptic to convulsions—he can't help it.

(202) If only one mistake were made in a hundred convictions and death sentences, society could not afford to make that mistake. You and I may blunder, but the state cannot afford the brutality of capital punishment as long as the convicted criminal is certainly anomalous, possibly diseased. The place for transgressors is the place of safekeeping. Let us have done with killing. Let us see to it that the new century may have no reason to look upon our shortsighted barbarism as we review with painful awe the century of the torturer and witch-burner.

(53) According to these principles, individuals deprived of free will should not be punished, but treated morally; individuals who possess free will, and who at the same time freely commit faults, should be punished, in spite of their sincere regret, for these punishments are merited.

(75) "It is a bad quarter of an hour to pass," said Cartouche in speaking of his approaching execution.

(161) The natural striving of men is to obtain the most frequent, intensive, and long-enduring happiness.

(161) The supreme question is, as to whether the world unrolls fatally, so that man has no more influence over his destiny than over the course of the stars; or, is a part of the plan of the world adapted to liberty, the knowledge of which imposes action.

(4) You want to tell her about how when you were just a little kid you used to think the moon followed you. In fact, you open your mouth and you are about to say that very thing, but you don't. Because it would be a lie. The truth is that you still think that the moon follows you. And you always will...and that makes you believe. You believe that this is real.

The Moon.

Grant Jerkins is the author of *A Very Simple Crime*, *At the End of the Road*, *The Ninth Step*, and *Done In One*. He lives in the Atlanta area with his wife and son. Visit his website at www.grantjerkins.com.

OTHER TITLES FROM DOWN AND OUT BOOKS

See www.DownAndOutBooks.com for complete list

By J.L. Abramo
Catching Water in a Net
Clutching at Straws
Counting to Infinity
Gravesend
Chasing Charlie Chan
Circling the Runway
Brooklyn Justice

By Trey R. Barker
2,000 Miles to Open Road
Road Gig: A Novella
Exit Blood
Death is Not Forever
No Harder Prison

By Richard Barre
The Innocents
Bearing Secrets
Christmas Stories
The Ghosts of Morning
Blackheart Highway
Burning Moon
Echo Bay
Lost

By Eric Beetner (editor)
Unloaded

By Eric Beetner and
JB Kohl
Over Their Heads

By Eric Beetner and
Frank Scalise
The Backlist
The Shortlist

By G.J. Brown
Falling

By Rob Brunet
Stinking Rich

By Mark Coggins
No Hard Feelings

By Tom Crowley
Vipers Tail
Murder in the Slaughterhouse

By Frank De Blase
Pine Box for a Pin-Up
Busted Valentines
and Other Dark Delights
A Cougar's Kiss

By Les Edgerton
The Genuine, Imitation,
Plastic Kidnapping

By A.C. Frieden
Tranquility Denied
The Serpent's Game
The Pyongyang Option (*)

By Jack Getze
Big Numbers
Big Money
Big Mojo
Big Shoes

By Richard Godwin
Wrong Crowd
Buffalo and Sour Mash (*)

(*)—Coming Soon

OTHER TITLES FROM DOWN AND OUT BOOKS

See www.DownAndOutBooks.com for complete list

By William Hastings (editor)
*Stray Dogs: Writing
from the Other America*

By Jeffery Hess
Beachhead

By Matt Hilton
No Going Back
Rules of Honor
The Lawless Kind
The Devil's Anvil

By David Housewright
Finders Keepers
Full House

By Jerry Kennealy
Screen Test

By Ross Klavan, Tim O'Mara and
Charles Salzberg
Triple Shot

By S.W. Lauden
Crosswise

By Terrence McCauley
The Devil Dogs of Belleau Wood

By Bill Moody
Czechmate
The Man in Red Square
Solo Hand
The Death of a Tenor Man
The Sound of the Trumpet
Bird Lives!

By Gary Phillips
The Perpetrators
Scoundrels (Editor)
Treacherous
3 the Hard Way

By Tom Pitts
Hustle

By Robert J. Randisi
Upon My Soul
Souls of the Dead
Envy the Dead (*)

By Ryan Sayles
The Subtle Art of Brutality
Warpath

By John Shepphird
The Shill
Kill the Shill
Beware the Shill (*)

By Ian Thurman
Grand Trunk and Shearer (*)

James R. Tuck (editor)
Mama Tried vol. 1
Mama Tried vol. 2 (*)

By Lono Waiwaiole
Wiley's Lament
Wiley's Shuffle
Wiley's Refrain
Dark Paradise
Leon's Legacy (*)

(*)—Coming Soon

Manufactured by Amazon.com
Columbia, SC
30 March 2017